Forbidden Obsession
Boneless Redemption Duet Book One

Isabella Alexander

Dedication

To you reading Forbidden Obsession: thank you for taking this trip on the wild side with me. I hope you enjoy this mafia romance. Happy reading!

This book contains profanity, nudity, descriptions of sexual acts, and graphic murder. Read at your own risk.

1

New York City

Dominic

Tap! Tap! Tap! Tap! Tap! Tap!

Priest Benjamin White ran across the cathedral breathlessly to escape me. His shoes echoed off the floors, and I could hear his frantic murmuring, undoubtedly saying his prayers.

Blending into the shadows of a darkened corridor, I watched him glance over his shoulder, his feet picking up speed. He thought he was running away from me.

Instead, he ran toward me.

I'd left a single black rose at the foot of the confessional door. When he exited and saw the rose, the dread that filled his face sucked away the blood in his veins, practically turning him into a ghost—pale and frozen in time.

He knew what the rose meant.

It was his time to die.

News of the Black Rose—a name given to me by people nationwide—had crossed every news circuit globally.

Some saw me as a threat to civilization. Others thought I was a vigilante since the people I went after were a detriment to their communities. The Lucas Cosa Nostra saw me as an enemy that needed to be taken down, dead or alive, because I used their signature black rose at the scenes of my crimes.

I was, in fact, all those things simultaneously. Most importantly, I was Dominic Lucas, heir to the boss Dameon Lucas, and underboss of the Lucas Cosa Nostra familia.

I'd singlehandedly run them all in circles and was the only one who knew the truth. And the truth was, I was angry as hell to be born into a life where my purpose was to do the very thing the people I sought and killed did—be a menace to society because of Dameon's criminal underworld.

For my own amusement, I made it my mission to erase the scum who'd been instrumental in the Lucas Cosa Nostra expansion—one death at a time.

During the day, I was an academic advisor at Manhattan Excellence & Arts University.

By night, I became the grim reaper.

PRIEST BENJAMIN WHITE scuffled around the corner and collided with my solid frame, crashing into me like a brick wall.

"Oh!" Frightened eyes crept up at me, his body shaken, as he took a step back.

"Hmmmmmmm," I growled, dressed in all black, my gloved fingers fisted, and my body radiating heat.

"Please, please," he begged.

I shut my eyes, inhaled a breath, and smirked, knowing when I reopened them the priest would have taken off into a sprint in the opposite direction.

Like clockwork, when I opened my eyes, he was gone. I sucked my teeth, stepped out of the shadows, and waited until he thought he could escape me before sending a blade flying across the cathedral where it sliced through his left shoulder and nailed him to the confessional doorframe.

"Aaaaaaaaaaaah!"

His echoing screams were like praise hymns to my ears. I took my time crossing the same path he'd taken, while he begged and pleaded for his life.

"Please, sir, sir, sir. I didn't do anything. I'm innocent! You can't do this! Vengeance is mine, saith the Lord!"

I paused in front of him and removed a hatchet from a

tool belt around my waist. His eyes widened as horror etched across his face, his body vibrating against the door as fear rose inside him.

"I am the Lord's vengeance."

He shit his pants within seconds of the hatchet's blade slicing through his throat. It was a quick death for him— quicker than the ones before him. That was all the mercy I had for the priest.

Yanking the weapon free, I grabbed his head and chopped twice more to remove his head from his body. His corpse dropped to the cathedral floor, and I removed a spike from my belt and impaled his head. Then I buried the bottom of the stake in a potted plant that sat on the cathedral doorsteps.

***

Corniquea Hills Suburbs

A FLICKER of light gave me pause as I turned into the driveway of my three-story mansion. But I knew the intruder inside my home was friend and not foe. To even enter Corniquea Hills, a retina scan was mandatory. The suburbs housed politicians, capos, and me—the underboss. Security was tighter than the Pentagon, and unless you carried someone's head who had access it was impossible to get inside.

I hit the button on the garage door, and when it lifted, a black sports car rested in my parking space.

Dameon—my father.

I inhaled, checked the time, and pulled into the vacant spot reserved for guests.

I exited the car and slammed the door, now dressed in a dark gray short-sleeved crew neck T-shirt, blue jeans that rode my solid cut hips, and dark gray buckled combat boots. The bloody black gear I had worn for my visit to the cathedral had already been discarded and burned.

The side door was unlocked, and when I entered, I quickly assessed the area, noting the three soldiers standing in the room's dark corners.

I didn't address them. Instead, I moved through the kitchen, entered the corridor, and moved into the sitting area where I took notice of Dameon's *consigliere*, Rolando Massimo, sitting on the navy contemporary sofa. In my chair, Dameon sat, smoking a cigar, as his eyes perused me. When I spoke to him, I addressed him as *Father* out of respect, but away from the Lucas Cosa Nostra, I referred to him as Dameon.

"You missed dinner," he said, his voice gruff as if he had a cough stuck in his throat.

I sucked my teeth. "Did you need to visit me with Rolando at your side, Father?"

Dameon's brows rose, and he released a puff of smoke. "What is the problem here?"

"Yes," Rolando drawled, "I would like to know the same."

I held my eyes on Dameon. "When you visit your heir, shouldn't you come as a father and not a boss?"

"Are you saying—"

"I'm not speaking to you, Rolando," I cut in. He closed his lips, his gaze dropping into a glare.

"You see," I added, returning my attention to Dameon. "I can't have a single conversation with you without his intrusion. Secondly, I would be forever grateful if you didn't bring your men into my home. You are safe as soon as you cross the threshold. You don't need them when visiting me."

Dameon held his stare on me, nodding, then spoke to Rolando. "Clear the house."

"Dameon..."

He peered at Rolando, and the man closed his mouth, stood, and exited the room. I waited until I heard the side door close, then I gave Dameon a smirk.

"Thank you."

He nodded once and pulled on his cigar. "What is with you and him lately?"

I kept my face neutral and sat in a chair across from him.

"There is nothing with me. I don't know what is

happening with him as I do not keep up with his disposition."

Laughter flew from Dameon's lips, followed by a rough cough. I peered at him, watched him gather himself after the rough spasm, then we sat in silence for a full minute.

"Are you okay?"

He mumbled. "Yeah." He cleared his throat. "Where have you been?"

My brows rose. "Fucking a woman I met last night."

He sniffed and perused me again. "You didn't discard her at yesterday's end?"

"She has some good pussy. I wanted more."

His rough laughter was back. "Discard her after tonight. Find someone else with good pussy."

"Do you think, at this point in my life, any woman has the tenacity to infiltrate my world with pussy, father?"

"Don't underestimate women."

"Don't underestimate me."

We stared at one another. If he had any idea how seriously he should take that statement, he would.

Dameon's lips spread. "You're my pride and joy. I don't underestimate you at all. I know what you're capable of, and you've made me proud." He drew on his cigar, held the smoke, and then released it. "You were supposed to eat with me tonight. You can fuck bimbos anytime. Don't let it happen again."

"As you wish, Father."

He nodded, rose to his feet, and extinguished his cigar in a glass ashtray.

"Walk me to the door."

We moved through my house, and at the side door, he grabbed my shoulder and turned his eyes to me.

"You're the only one I trust. Remember that."

"More than Rolando?"

"More than any fuckin' one."

We held each other's gazes, then I nodded.

"I need you to stay vigilant and keep your ears to the streets. We need to find out who this fucker is, the one imitating our signature."

I nodded again. "I will eventually find him."

"Dinner, tomorrow. Don't be late."

"Yes, sir."

I watched him leave, saw Rolando glare at me through the car window, then shut the blinds and headed for a shower.

2

Dominic

Traffic was light on campus as the day neared its end. The weather in Manhattan had been cold as frequent storms buffeted the area lately. Today, the sky was dim, and cool shards of wind whipped across my face as I crossed the yard, headed to the campus library.

My career as an academic advisor was the perfect cover. It kept me in a favorable light since everyone knew who Dameon was, that I was his son, and that his billionaire status meant he must've screwed over his workers to build his empire to the level it was.

The truth was simple—he was the boss of the Lucas Cosa Nostra. His illegal businesses escalated him to billionaire status. The billiard clubs, casinos, and health-care facilities were props. He was okay with letting the public assume he overworked his employees, ran sweatshops, and paid unfair wages rather than have them know the truth.

In the eyes of the citizens, my career made me the do-gooder. The one who refused to be a part of Dameon's shady empire by building my own life the way I saw fit but, most importantly, out of his shadow.

I smirked as I strolled toward the door of the library. In another life—one where I'd chosen my destiny—this would've been my reality. And though the world around me was real, my reality was as dark as the pits of hell.

"Mr. Lucas!"

I paused, turned, and smiled at the young man running toward me. Anthony Drone was a freshman filled with hopes and dreams and had yet to be tainted by the world's ugly truths. Lucky him.

"Mr. Drone."

"Hey, sorry, didn't mean to bother you, but I was thinking about what you said earlier. About the time it would take away from my studies if I switched classes in the middle of my semester versus choosing the appropriate courses to take now."

I nodded.

"Well, you're right. During my senior year in high school, I considered what I wanted to do with my life. A doctor and lawyer were right up there at the top. But I didn't consider the elective studies I'd have to take. I want to thank you for drilling it down and helping me think about that. Those classes are important, too. Who knows how they'll help in my future?"

I nodded again. "I'm glad I could be of service, Anthony." He nodded and slipped his glasses up his nose, and hesitated. "Is there anything else?"

"Uh...no." He paused. "One last thing." I stared at him, unmoving. "You're my hero, Mr. Lucas."

I blinked once and frowned. "Excuse me?"

He laughed nervously. "Yeah. I know you come from a wealthy family. So do I, and I admire you for breaking the mold and taking your career into your own hands. Just wanted to let you know that." A goofy laugh dropped from him. "I did the same. So, thank you for that, too."

He was serious.

Anthony bounced his lean weight from one leg to the other. "All right then, I'll let you go. Have a good day, Mr. Lucas."

He turned and jogged away as fast as he'd come, and I gritted my teeth and fisted my fingers as anger moved through me.

"If only that had been the case, Anthony," I murmured. The urge to kill again hit me in the center of my gut. Usually, once I'd removed one of the marks on my list, I would be satisfied for a few months before I needed to do it again.

But hearing Anthony's cheerful praise reignited the ire inside me. I slipped my hand into my pants pocket and gripped the small but necessary stress ball I kept on hand. I'd noticed long ago that repeatedly squeezing and releasing the foam orb helped me calm myself when necessary.

Taking a deep breath, I shut my eyes and exhaled, then turned, and entered the library.

"Mr. Lucas." The attendant greeted me with a nod. "It's late evening. Is there anything I can help you with?"

Sandra Tillerman was a sixty-eight-year-old veteran who worked at the school library. Usually, she had someone caught in conversation when I came in, sharing stories about her time in the United States Army.

"I'm here to drop off a few books and be on my way. How are you, Ms. Tillerman?" Her face brightened, her green eyes sparkled, and her silver hair bounced when she moved.

"Wonderful. I couldn't be better. Although, the weather could be better. Some days I'm unsure whether to wear a jacket."

"Whenever you're confused about it, always wear a jacket. You'd rather not need it than be cold, hmm?"

She nodded in agreement. "You're right. Always right."

I offered her a polite smile. "Have a good day, Ms. Tillerman."

"You do the same, Mr. Lucas."

Turning to leave, my eyes scanned the room and ran into a cascade of golden-brown curls. I paused, and blinked, my gaze riding over the lean silhouette I knew to be Penelope Cattaneo. Our introduction had been somewhat unusual—she'd been struck by a speeding bicyclist as she crossed the campus street two months ago, and the glancing blow sent her flying onto the hood of my car.

Initially, I was incensed, annoyed, and biting back curses when I exited the vehicle. Then I saw her—strikingly gorgeous, with mystic golden irises, butterscotch skin, and that wavy, fluffy mermaid hair.

My attraction to Penelope was instant, and when she'd gathered herself to look at me, I knew the attraction hit her the same way if her relentless flirting was any indication.

After the school nurse saw to Penelope's bruises, she laid across my office couch staring at me. She'd gone from resting, to perching her ass on my desk.

PENELOPE'S *citrus scent hit my nose, her nearness profound and doing an odd thing to my sudden arousal.*

"Don't be scared," she whispered. "No one would have to know about us, but us...and besides, we've got an alibi as to why I'm here. The nurse is our witness."

She reached down, her fingers touching my shirt when I reacted, rising to my feet, and gripping her throat in the palm of one hand.

OUR SHORT TIME together ended with me teaching Penelope a lesson. At least, that's what I'd thought I did by instilling fear into her. The truth was, I could dive into Penelope's world, fuck her relentlessly, adore her tirelessly, then throw her away when my excitement for her waned.

But now was not the time for distractions. I had to remain focused on my primary goal—to tear down the Lucas Cosa Nostra, one death at a time. Getting involved with Penelope in any way was a interference I couldn't bear to risk. She was a student, and it was forbidden to act on any unethical desires I had for her.

The goal was to keep curious eyes off me—to maintain a clean reputation so I could complete my mission in peace. Fucking a student would definitely impede my progress. With this knowledge, there was no reason for me to stand still, watching her from across the room. Yet I was a statue, my blood warm and my pulse rising the longer I assessed her. What was it about Penelope that made my feet move into a slow stroll? Heading in her direction, I felt out of control.

I paused and glanced at a row of books just as she glanced over her shoulder. I imagined Penelope's golden irises dilating when she saw me—imagined her pulse rocking in her neck, her heart accelerating, her pussy clenching, her clitoris thumping wildly as desire surged between her thighs.

I pretended not to notice her stare, slipped my hands inside the pocket of my Ferragamo slacks, and moved away from her. Slowly, I neared the end of the row, and her figure appeared at the opposite end I'd just walked from. I held back a smirk. There she was, observing me, still curious, even when a part of her soul feared me.

When she had tried to seduce me in my office, I'd grabbed her by her throat, planted her against the wall, and cut the flow to her oxygen with the strength in my fingers. It was enough to make her run away from me; I needed her to fear me. But here Penelope was, following me as I strolled row to row, pretending to look for a book that didn't exist.

I turned left and went down an aisle that took us further away from the front of the library. When I'd gotten further enough away, I paused, lifted a book suddenly, then turned and ran into her.

"Oh!"

I gripped her arm to keep her balance. My forehead creased as I squinted, my nostrils flaring as her citrusy scent hit me like a Mac truck. Heat ran down my body straight to my dick, and I locked my jaw, inhaled, and exhaled—trying to release the craving that filled my bones.

"Ms. Cattaneo."

"That is you," she responded, her voice filled with dark desire.

"It is. And it's you, too."

She smiled, but it quickly faded. "Yes." She cleared her throat, lingered, and her gaze covered the full length of me under a sweep of her fluttering lashes. Penelope was trying to get a feel for me, to see if I was the scary monster who'd run her from my office, or if I was the calm advisor I'd been known as around campus.

"Excuse me, Ms. Cattaneo. I didn't see you."

"Oh, it's my fault."

My brows arched. "Were you following me?"

"Uh..." she smiled, and the gesture upended the surge in my heartbeat.

"Following is such an invasive term."

"Oh, yeah?"

My gaze dropped to her pouty mouth, and I traveled through a naughty visual of me shoving my dick down her throat. Yearning hit me in my gut again, and I locked my jaw and attempted to control my libido.

"Yeah. I prefer to call it curiosity."

"Curiosity killed the cat, Penelope."

She sucked in an audible breath as my reference must've brought her back to our initial meeting and what happened when I'd responded the same way. My brows dipped, and my gaze stroked her from head to toe.

Blue jeans fitted her figure, hugging her curvy hips, and she wore red ankle boots on her feet. The blouse was a soft blush color. It was short sleeved and revealed the tattoo between her arm of a caterpillar morphing into a butterfly. Her jewelry—a gold necklace, bracelets, teardrop earrings, three rings on one finger and two on the other—highlighted her striking features.

"Goddess."

Her brows rose, and pleasure ripped through her face. "What?"

I held steady. I'd misspoken, which never happened, but I reiterated because I could own up to my mistakes.

"I said, you're a goddess, Penelope." Inhaling her scent, I let the aroma linger between my nostrils longer than I should've. "Excuse me." I stepped around her. It was time to get away from Penelope.

"Professor!"

I paused, her desire to call me *professor* instead of *advisor* arousing me as if she'd licked up my shaft.

I looked back at her, and she walked up behind me. "You can't just tell me I'm a goddess and leave." Her voice was laced with yearning.

I turned to face her. "Yes, I can."

Her eyes twinkled. "No, you can't."

"Who's going to stop me, Penelope?"

She raised an eyebrow. "You don't seem to be moving."

I turned again, and she grabbed my arm, clutching my bicep in her soft grip. My eyes dropped to her fingers, then back at her.

"You shouldn't touch me, Penelope."

"Why? Are you going to choke me out again?"

I sucked in a breath and faced her fully. "You want answers. Is that why you've followed me down this aisle?"

Her eyes widened. "Yes and no." She stumbled over her words. "You just admitted it."

My brows rose. "You're surprised."

"Yeah, because..." she shrugged, "...what if my intentions were to get you to own up to what you did to me? You could lose your job." She snapped her fingers. "Like that."

I smirked. She was feisty. That only made me want to dig my fingers into her flesh, grip her hard, and fuck her against a bookcase.

"Are you recording me, Penelope?"

"What?"

She appeared confused as if she hadn't offered a possible threat. I eased closer to her, closing the gap between us.

"Have you followed me to record my admittance to choking you so you can report me to the dean?"

She frowned, then relaxed her face. "No. But...but... that's not the point."

"Then what is?"

"I'm just surprised you admitted it so fast. If I weren't someone who liked you, I might have ruined your life."

Dark laughter, low and vibrational, dropped from my lips.

She quivered. "What's so funny?"

"I can assure you, Penelope, nothing you or anyone else does can ruin me."

She swallowed, and her eyes were stuck on mine. My voice changed—the nocturnal sound, the timbre I reserved for those who were taking their last breaths.

"I fear no man, Penelope. Do you understand me?"

She saw the shift in my demeanor, remembered it from our last meeting, and the fear I expected her to feel returned to her face.

I lifted a hand to her chin, lightly touched her with the tips of my fingers, smiled, and then turned to leave.

Penelope took in a sharp breath. "I'll be at Romeo's tonight to let my hair down. You should stop by if you're into that sort of thing," she rushed to announce.

I paused again but didn't look back, and instead, moved from the row to get as far away from Penelope as I could.

Before I did something that I would regret.

3

Dominic

T he sky was a deep shade of navy when I arrived at Dameon's compound. Shrouded in a veil of darkness, the cold winter weather nipped at my skin.

Security at the entrance was tight, as expected. Despite the biting cold, I was greeted by the sight of Dameon's loyal guards standing watch outside the gate. I passed through the iron gates without being stopped and walked through the compound. The gardens were barren, and the fountains were frozen over. The cold weather had taken its toll on everything, including the staff. The few servants that were present outside were huddled together in heavy coats, their breaths visible in the frigid air.

THE MAIN BUILDING was a sprawling mansion, with a mix of modern and traditional architecture. I walked up the stone path that led to the entrance of the Lucas Estate, the crunch of snow under my feet announcing my arrival.

Inside, I strolled the long corridor and removed my boots before entering Dameon's quarters. I was greeted by the warm glow of a roaring fire in the hearth.

Dameon was seated in his favorite armchair, surrounded by his closest advisors. He looked up as I entered and gave me a curt nod of acknowledgement, but frustration, and anger riddled his facial features.

THE ROOM WAS FILLED with the mouth-watering aroma of roasted lamb, which the chef had prepared for dinner. There was also a pot of hot soup and a platter of fresh bread on the table. The walls were adorned with family portraits and antique paintings, and the décor was traditional and elegant.

"Dominic, my son, welcome," he said, biting back a snarl.

"Thank you, Father." I took a seat opposite him.

A servant approached the table and placed servings of food on our plates.

"You appear angry. What did I miss?"

He waited until the servers exited the room before he spoke.

"The priest." He grimaced, then spoke to Rolando. "Show him."

Rolando lifted a remote and powered on a flat screen television against the wall.

Images of the cathedral, surrounded with yellow tape, and reporters announcing their breaking news filled the screen. Rolando flipped from one news outlet to the next. CNN, Fox-News, local and national circuits were spinning the same story behind different faces.

"Fifteen hundred pounds of *cocaina* sits in that cathedral's basement."

He took in a breath, then shouted, "*Millecinquecento!*" His tirade continued in our native language.

"*Did you hear me?*" His eyes scanned each man in the room. "*Fifteen hundred pounds!*" Dameon slammed his fist on the tabletop and the utensils jingled. "*There is no motherfuckin' reason that this killing fucker should have gotten the priest! How the fuck did this happen?*"

I matched his tongue and responded in Italian. "*Who was White's security?*"

"*Gianni,*" Rolando offered.

I cut my eyes at Rolando. "*He was someone under your command, correct?*"

Rolando sucked his teeth. "*He's gone missing.*"

My brows rose and I looked at the surprise on Dameon's face.

"*What the fuck do you mean, gone missing?*" Dameon barked.

"In the last twenty-four hours he's gone radio-silent. I've sent capos to his home and he's not there."

"Why the fuck are you just now telling me this?"

"I was in the midst of handling it myself."

"You're doing a great fuckin' job of that!"

I smirked and shook my head, catching Rolando's glare. *"If you've got something to say, figlio, say it now."*

"I'm not your son. So never address me as such." I turned my attention to Dameon. *"I'll find out what happened to Gianni. In the meantime, you should think about changing up the guards, their shifts, and who they protect. I feel the soldiers have gotten complacent. No one has gotten this close to our immediate allies. It's time to switch things up."*

"How has no one gotten this close when some of our top allies have been removed from this earthly plane?"

Rolando's challenge was something I should've been used to. Since I was of age, he'd added his two cents to every issue, intended to overrule me at every turn, and my annoyance regarding him had grown into suspicion. If I hadn't been the Black Rose, I would've thought it was him. The power Dameon had given him had gone to his head and he was bloodthirsty for it now.

"They were not directly working for us, were they?"

"Still—"

"Then like I said...the guards have gotten complacent. This is the last thing we need, considering someone is targeting the Cosa Nostra."

"My son is right," Dameon cut in. *"Change up the guards immediately."* He turned his eyes to me. *"Find Gianni."*

I nodded and Dameon said a prayer over the food. Silently we ate. But while everyone was most likely thinking of the priest and Gianni's whereabouts, my thoughts bounced between how long I would let Gianni remain tied up in the locked shed outside Rolando's home.

And Penelope.

———

"If I weren't someone who liked you, I might have ruined your life."

The question that boggled my mind was why. Why did Penelope "like" me?

As I left Dameon's compound, these thoughts remained as I drove the dark streets.

"I'll be at Romeo's tonight to let my hair down. You should stop by if you're into that sort of thing."

At the light, I made a U-turn and headed across town to Romeo's.

Wracked with indecision, I gritted my teeth, annoyed with the constant need to satiate this desire for Penelope that burned inside me.

"I won't approach her," I told myself firmly.

I checked the rearview mirror after convincing myself I was there to merely observe. One way or the other, it had to happen. Penelope had managed to get my attention, and once that occurred, I had to commit myself to the person or task until I was satisfied.

Instead of valet parking, I parked in the club garage, took the elevator down, and entered Romeo's. Neon lights swung overhead as I made my way through the throngs of people. The music was loud and pounding, the neon lights blinding, and the air thick with the scent of alcohol, cheap perfume, and sweat.

"Penelope. Penelope," I whispered.

She was the sole reason I resisted the urge to slip away to my usual haunts as I ventured into this seedy nightclub.

People were drinking, some holding beer bottles, others sipping colorful cocktails through straws. The bartenders were in a frenzy, shaking and pouring drinks at lightning speed. The energy was electric, and the music was loud. I could feel the bass vibrating through my chest. Patrons eager to dance were crowding onto the dance floor, pushing and shoving past the tables.

I kept to the shadows, my dark, brooding presence unnoticed by the revelers around me. I wasn't one for conversation or socializing; tonight was no exception. I was here to survey, observe, and take in every detail of Penelope's movements, every nuance of her smile.

The club was packed with people, all dressed to impress and ready to party. There were girls in short, tight dresses and heels that looked impossible to walk in and guys in designer suits and slicked-back hair. It seemed to me they were all here for the same reason—to escape their mundane lives and lose themselves in the pulsing beat of the music.

The sounds were a mix of electronic beats and bass-heavy rhythms. The dance floor was a sea of bodies moving in perfect unison to the beat.

Then she came into view, standing at the bar, looking as beautiful as ever.

Penelope.

My heart skipped a beat as I watched her order a drink, her long golden-brown hair falling in soft waves around her shoulders.

A guy approached her, his hands reaching to pull her toward him. Jealousy rose in my chest, and his hands roamed over her body and cupped her ass.

She wiggled away from his touch, and as I gritted my teeth, my gaze followed them around the room's wall to the dance floor. Penelope's body gyrated in perfect sync with the music, and he tried to pick up her groove, but it was clear he possessed two left feet.

I couldn't tear my eyes away, even though I knew I should. She was like a drug to me, a sweet addiction I couldn't resist.

And so, I stayed, observing in the shadows as the night wore on. Penelope moved from the dance floor to the bar, then back again. She laughed with her friends, her smile lighting up the room. And even though I knew I shouldn't have her, even though I knew it was forbidden—desire washed over me, slammed into my libido, and gripped my dick.

Like an animal to its prey, I was unable to tear myself away from the magnetic pull that beckoned me across the room.

That same fella hung on to her like his life depended on it. I knew he intended to keep paying for her drinks in the hopes that she would leave with him, if only it were to fuck her on the backseat of his car or take her to a hotel.

He whispered in her ear, and she leaned away, turned her face up to look at him, and shook her head no.

He frowned, grabbed her ass, and his lips curved in a sinister smirk when he whispered again, no doubt issuing threats or something crass.

The pulse in my throat thumped, my hands fisted, and my gut tightened. As expected, he made the wrong move, yanking Penelope toward him as she pushed him away.

Their voices grew and eyes turned toward them as partygoers looked to see what the fuss was about.

As for me, I was halfway across the club, my hurried strides lengthening as she slapped him across the face. He lifted a hand to return her assault when I snatched him up by his collar, yanked him away from her, and dropped him to the ground.

"What the fuck, man!"

I hated when people addressed me as "man." It was rude and diminished a person's worth to the measly definition of wretched humanity.

"I'm not your fuckin' man," I snarled.

He jumped to his feet and lifted a finger in my face. "You should mind your business and get the fuck out of my—" I grabbed his finger and snapped it before he spit out his threat.

"Aaaaaaaaaaaaah!"

Nostrils flaring, I clutched the back of his neck. "What were you going to do, hmm? Drag her out of the club kicking and screaming?" I slapped him across his face, and his face turned beet red.

"Did you plan to rape her?" I slapped him again, so hard I left a bright red mark from my palm across his face. "Speak, you son of a bitch."

"No! No!"

"What's wrong? You sound distressed. Respect the ladies and watch your motherfuckin' mouth when you speak to me, or I'll rip your tongue out and feed it to my pit bulls."

I slapped him a final time and released him, and his body crashed to the floor. Whining and wounded, he rolled from his back to his stomach, climbed unsteadily to his knees, and hurriedly dragged himself away from us.

A soft hand grabbed my bicep, and a string of heat slipped through my body. I turned, and Penelope's wide-eyed attention knocked me back into reality.

"You came." Her eyes lit up, and pleasure moved through her features as her lips curved.

I touched her chin with the tip of my fingers. "Pretend you didn't see me."

Turning away from Penelope, I walked through the crowd. My plans were to escape her, and the prying eyes now aimed in our direction, wondering who the man was who'd just saved the girl.

I was uninterested in their curiosity and needed to keep a low profile. That was almost impossible in today's times as people clung to their phones and electronics like extra body parts.

I pushed my shoulder into the exit, entered the garage, and stepped into a waiting elevator. The doors closed as a figure darted through them, almost getting caught. She collided with my chest.

Penelope.

The doors hesitated, then closed, and I gritted my teeth and glared at her.

"What are you doing?"

"I'm going with you."

Frustration riddled me. "Get out, Penelope."

"No."

We had a stare-down, and I reached for the open-door button when she swatted my hand away. I snarled, the sound a warning.

"I don't care about your dark growls or wolfish snarls, professor. I don't think you'll hurt me."

"Are you sure about that?"

She bit back her response but kept her head high and

lips puckered. I wanted to grab her, kiss her mouth, suck her tongue, and then gag her with my erection.

"Get the fuck out, Penelope."

"No, professor!"

"Don't call me professor in this setting, Penelope."

"Don't tell me to get out then, Dominic."

Hearing my name fall from her lips aroused me even more.

"Damn it..." I hit the button that took me to the floor where my vehicle was parked. A smugly satisfied smile etched across her lips.

"You didn't win."

"Looks like I did."

I drew in a heavy breath. "What do you want?"

"To hang out."

"To hang out?" I shook my head.

"Why do you sound like I'm being ridiculous?"

"Does it look like I hang out, Penelope?"

Her eyes covered me. "Actually, in a dark, sexy, devilish kinda way."

I turned my body to face her and closed the air between us as she backpedaled—trapped against the tin wall.

"Is that the kind of fun you like, Penelope?"

She shivered and bit her bottom lip. "With you."

Deep laughter fell from me. "If you knew what you were asking for, you'd take those words back."

"I'm not a unicorn, you know. It doesn't take a rocket

scientist to know you've got an edge about you that you keep hidden."

My brows rose. "And how would you assume something like that?"

"You're Dameon Lucas's son. Even if you're the better part of him, his blood still runs in your veins, and he's notorious for being a bad guy."

I stared at her. She was right, and that angered me. Every time I was reminded of the blood that ran through me, it was a reminder that there was nothing on this earthly plane I could do to escape my destiny.

An unintentional growl escaped me.

"I'm nothing like Dameon."

"I didn't say you were like him, per se." Her hands slipped up my chest. "I can tell you're the better half of him." Her hands caressed my neck, my face, and desire dug into my core as I stared into those beautiful eyes.

"You have no idea who I am."

"Then show me who you are."

"Why would I do that?"

"Because I want to know you and you want to know me."

I glared at her. "If I wanted to know you, I could find out in thirty seconds."

Her eyes widened. "How?"

"You're full of questions, aren't you?"

"I want to know everything about you, Dominic."

Heat slid down my skin and the nerves in my body were hyperaware of her touch.

"There's no reason to fill yourself with that information."

"Why?"

"Why?" I mocked. "There is no purpose behind such an invasion."

"We could be friends, and..." she shrugged, "...maybe more."

"Penelope. You are a student at the institution I work for. If there are cameras in this elevator, the evidence could destroy my career. Do you want that?"

"You said nothing could ruin you."

My lips spread into a smile. *Ah, she listens.*

"Penelope."

"To answer your question, no. But no one has to know about us."

"You're trouble."

"Kiss me, professor," she whispered.

I was tempted. So fuckin' tempted I listened to my dick instead of my brain and gripped her thighs, lifted her, and pushed my pelvis into her open legs.

"Penelope..."

"Yes. Just like this."

I nibbled up her jaw, smashed my lips into her mouth, and inhaled her tongue. Our bodies burst with fever as sensations fled down my skin and hers.

"Oooooh..."

The moan that slipped from her mouth made me press

harder into her and my dick pushed into her panties as I indulged in the flavor of her mouth.

Ding!

The elevator doors opened, and I dropped Penelope to her feet, exited quickly, and turned to stare at her as they closed promptly.

4

Penelope

The next day

He left me panting like a horny teenager inside that elevator.

A brief string of wind whipped around my face as I sat on the balcony of my condo the following day. It was too cold to sit outside in the open air, so I was thankful for the custom windows I had added to the outside deck. They shielded me from the harsh temperatures, whether intense heat or sharp, cool winds, while allowing me to relax outside and enjoy the view in relative comfort.

Today, my girls and I were having brunch, and they were chit-chatting away about campus parties and the jocks they planned to seduce. At the same time, all I could concentrate on was dark gray eyes, a strong jawline, a black beard and goatee, and an irresistibly spicy, pussy-throbbing scent that wrapped around me like a blanket.

I must have been out of my mind. Professor Lucas—or Dominic—had always been mysterious to me. Rumors around campus—depending on who you heard them from —made him out to be either a friendly do-gooder or a dark prince. Over the last four years at Manhattan Excellence & Arts University, I focused mainly on my studies and only daydreamed about what type of person Professor Lucas might be.

But now it was clear to me that Dominic and Professor Lucas were two different people. While Professor Lucas was quite possibly the do-gooder, Dominic was unstable.

I found that out the hard way when he snatched me off my feet and choked me out in his office. Looking into his eyes that day twisted my guts. It was as if he'd revealed a darkness inside of him that awakened my curiosity.

Adding to that, he'd almost killed me.

That day, I lost the fight to fill my lungs with oxygen, and he didn't seem to flinch while watching me desperately writhing, trying to breathe. Someone with some good sense would've run away and never looked back. For a moment, I considered it.

But a part of me wanted to know why he'd done it, and I admit I wondered what it was like to have such power— to send someone fleeing like the devil was on their heels.

A few months had passed since I last saw Professor

Lucas, but when he manifested in the campus library, I'd felt knocked off my feet at his appearance. His black button-down shirt and pants fit him as if tailored to his hard body. His strides held a sexy flair that kept my eyes stuck on his movements. To say I was aroused by him at every turn was an understatement.

Last night he saved me from having to physically fight off a man who thought he owned me because he'd bought me a few drinks.

What a loser.

It had all happened so fast that I didn't realize my heart was beating through my chest until Dominic left me in that elevator in silence.

Seeing him in my element, I hadn't mistaken the desire in his gaze, nor had I misunderstood the passion with which he kissed me.

And now he owned me because I could never let go of this feeling that we were fated somehow.

"SNAP, SNAP, EARTH TO PENELOPE!"

I blinked, pushed back my thoughts, and Emma, Sofia, and Alice came into focus.

"What happened?"

They all looked at each other, then back at me.

"Where have you been?" Emma asked. She was the first to befriend me when I made my debut as a freshman at Manhattan Excellence & Arts University. It must've been my lucky day because, according to most on campus, Emma didn't befriend people. People mostly wanted to befriend her since she was the mayor's daughter and the top socialite on the campus next to Sofia. The two hung on to each other's style and words and laughed like they were Siamese twins. Sofia was the daughter of Senator Darwin Willinger, and her mother was a city councilman.

Alice, on the other hand, was the police chief's daughter, and the three of them were like a cheerleading squad that everyone wanted to hang around. Men sought them out first. Girls did what was necessary to get their attention and show they were cool.

As for me, I was an observer who mostly kept to myself unless I was approached. If there was something I wanted, I went after it with tenacity. Most thought I was drop-dead gorgeous. Mix that with the fact that everyone knew my parents to be the Bonnie and Clyde of our time, and I was suddenly the next coolest person next to Emma, Sofia, and Alice.

Two sets of blue eyes and a pair of brown eyes stared back at me. Emma adjusted herself, and her blonde bob bounced across her shoulders.

"Are you going to tell us what you're thinking about?"

I smirked. "I'm thinking about what you just said."

Alice twisted her lips. "Don't play us for a fool. You weren't listening to anything we said."

"You were talking about the party at the fraternity house tomorrow night."

The three of them looked at each other, and Sofia mumbled. "Maybe she did hear us."

Emma nodded, and Alice slipped an autumn-brown strand of hair behind her ear.

"We still want to know what you were thinking about," Emma added.

I smirked and glanced at them all, then sipped my lemonade.

"I know you all have your pick of guys at school, but... have you ever considered fuckin' a professor?"

They gasped, eyes wide and mouths agape. Emma lifted her hands.

"Wait a minute." She thought it over. "We know every administrator at this school. No one is sexy enough to...."

Her words died. "Unless..." She shook her head. "No way."

Sofia grabbed her wrist. "You're not thinking who I'm thinking, are you?"

"I most certainly am."

I chuckled. "How would you know each other's thoughts unless you have some psychic capabilities you haven't told me about?"

"This would be new to me, too," Alice added.

Alice and I glanced at each other, then back to Emma and Sofia.

"We just know," Sofia said.

I was convinced Sofia was more excited about that than Emma, and it was my observation that Sofia would agree with whatever Emma said she thought.

"I've decided not to guess in case I'm wrong," Emma said finally. "You know I don't like being wrong."

I chuckled. "I never said I had someone in mind. But there are some cute professors at the school." I shrugged. "I just wondered if you three had ever considered seducing one."

"No, you said *fuckin'*. Seducing and fuckin' are two different things, honey."

I laughed at Alice. "How are they different?"

"Seducing is the foreplay to fuckin'. Fuckin' is *fuckin'*."

They all laughed, and I nodded in agreement. "Okay, you've got me there."

I lifted a fork and butter knife and cut into my pancake. I hadn't touched my food since we got out here, mainly because my focus was in one direction only—with Professor Lucas, Dominic, or whatever he wanted me to call him.

A part of me wanted to tell the girls what led me to the question. I hadn't told them about the incident in his office, library, or club. And while they were there with me last night, all three of them had been in the ladies' room when Dominic had appeared. By the time they came out, we were both gone, but they were so busy partying they'd yet to ask me where I disappeared to.

"I haven't thought much about the professors since Ethan Lancaster has my undivided attention!" Sofia shouted. She lifted her arms in the air, threw her head back, her curly blonde, shoulder length hair dropping down her back when she closed her eyes. A sigh slipped from her lips, and she shivered.

"That man is so gorgeous."

"Don't date him," I said.

She gasped and turned surprised eyes at me. "Why not?"

"Come on, Sofia," Alice moaned. "Everyone knows Ethan is a whore hopper."

Her face scrunched, and she dropped her hands. "Did you just call me a whore?"

Alice shook her head. "No. Absolutely not. Why would I do that?"

Sofia peered at her. "Well, why would you say that?"

"Because Ethan's a whore."

I held back a laugh because the more truth Alice spoke, the more frustration settled on Sofia's face. I hated that for her. She deserved better.

"Ethan is a plaything. Don't take him seriously," Emma advised.

Sofia gawked. "Not you too."

Emma stroked her arm and nodded. "You know we love you, so if we're telling you this, it's not because we don't want to see you happy. If you must give Ethan some attention, make him work for your pussy because once he gets it, he's gone."

"Do you really think he would do me like that?"

"What makes you any different than anyone else?"

She looked at me, horror-stricken. "Did you really just ask me that?"

Alice laughed, and I smirked and stuffed my mouth with more pancakes.

"Men have a level of not caring about who anyone is. Unless they want you as their wife. And we're in college. You should stick to reality. How many college men are looking for wives? And before you answer that, compare it to how many college men are looking for whores."

Sofia moaned. "Why must you shit on my hopes and dreams like this?" Her eyes widened and she pouted.

Alice sighed. "Would you rather we lie and say go for it, you'll be Mrs. Lancaster in no time?"

"Yes."

Alice and Emma laughed while I shook my head and swallowed my food. Grabbing a napkin, I wiped the corners of my mouth, took a sip of lemonade, and gave Sofia my attention.

"You would not. The first thing you'd do was ask what kind of friends we were not to stop your descent into love with a known pussy-rider."

Emma shrieked in laughter. "Pussy-rider! I've got to use that!"

Alice giggled, and Sofia pouted more.

"For the record, I do think there are some women men would guard their dicks around," Emma said.

Sofia looked at her with wide-eyed hope as Emma continued.

"Take Penelope, for example."

I choked on my pancake, and Alice patted me on the back. Clearing my throat, I blinked rapidly at Emma. "Excuse me?"

She nodded. "Yeah. Because of who your parents are. What man in his right mind would screw over someone with relatives known to bust a cap in your ass?"

Laughter pealed from Alice, and Sofia nodded as they all looked at me.

"Ha!" I shook my head. "Why would anyone be afraid of them? They're in an upstate prison. And they're not getting out anytime soon!"

Emma cursed. "Shit. With their track record, no one's going to test that out. I mean, how many boyfriends have you had cheat on you?"

"Quite a few, actually."

"Name them."

"I—" My mouth hung open as I went through the short list of men to whom I'd given my attention. Truth be told, they could hardly be called men; more like boys cosplaying as men.

Eric was too needy. He'd gotten on my nerves, following me around like a puppy so much that I had to break things off. I needed the reprieve. Alex was a chauvinist, and much like Sofia, I'd been too caught up in how sexy he was to notice it until it was too late. Then there was Braylen, who I thought was a chill guy until I realized he just didn't care much about anything. He had no ambitions or thoughts on whatever subject broached, Braylen had to go.

"We're waiting."

I glanced at Emma, then at Sofia and Alice. "They were...what, middle school, high school? I can't remember. The point is, my parents aren't scaring anybody."

Emma looked at Sofia. "Don't believe her. She's never had someone play with her in the four years we've all been in school together. Think about it. When any of the guys approach her, aren't they polite, well-spoken, and full of good mannerisms?"

Alice tapped her jaw, and Sofia peered at me.

"Yeaaaah." Sofia nodded. "You're right."

"Of course, you'd say that." My voice was sharper than I'd intended.

She frowned. "What is that supposed to mean?"

"Nothing."

"No, tell me."

I stared at her. "You agree with anything Emma says."

She dropped her curious peer. "Oh. Well, that's because she's always correct in her assessments, just as she is now."

"Thank you!" Emma chimed.

I pushed my lips out. "This is not about me. This is

about preventing you..." I placed a hand on Sofia's shoulder, "...from doing something you'll surely regret. Go on, have as much fun with Ethan as you want, but don't take him seriously."

Sofia sighed. "Sometimes I wish I were in your shoes."

I frowned. "Are you still on this?"

"No, seriously, Penelope."

"So you wish your parents were in prison?"

She frowned. "Well, of course not but—"

"That's exactly what it's like being in my shoes. The grass isn't greener on this side."

Sofia lifted her hand as if to stop me from continuing.

"Listen to me."

I closed my lips and let her proceed.

"You have this beautiful condo to yourself, your current guardian—"

"I'm an adult."

Sofia pursed her lips. "I know that."

"I don't have a guardian."

"You know what I mean. Your current parent is your uncle, who is low-key and doesn't bother you much. You have an unlimited source of income—"

"I never told you that."

Sofia pursed her lips. "You're not going to let me get through this, are you?"

I sighed. "Continue."

"You come and go as you please, can shop till you drop, have no ailments that we know of, and have men suck up to you at the drop of a dime. You can literally have anyone you want."

I opened my mouth, and Sofia held up a finger. Alice and Emma giggled, and I smirked.

"You are free. Do you understand? F. R. E. E." She pointed a red fingernail to herself. "Me, on the other hand, am watched constantly. Why? Because Darwin wants to make sure I don't embarrass him. Apparently, according to all of you, I can't get the man of my dreams—"

"Because he's a whore!" Alice inserted.

Sofia offered her a smug smile. "Yes, yes, let's not leave that out." She inhaled a deep breath. "On top of that, my credit card has a limit." Her frown deepened. "It's asinine, really."

I chuckled. "That's the real reason you're pouting, isn't it?"

"What?"

"The credit card limit."

Emma and Alice laughed, and Sofia twisted her lips. "It plays a big role. I won't lie. But," she lifted that red fingernail again, pointing in my direction. "Everything I said is valid. You're free, and I'm...me."

"Hey." I rubbed her forearm. "There's nothing wrong with being you, Sofia."

Her forehead creased, and her lip puckered. "Did you just hear what I said?"

"Yes. And you know what I heard? You have stability,

protection, and love. Call me crazy, but I'd rather have that any day."

Sofia's brows dipped as she thought it over.

Alice and Emma nodded.

"I love how you're able to see the bright side of life," Emma said. "It's just another thing to add to that long list of things Sofia said that makes you great."

I smiled. These girls really filled my heart with love. Sometimes it was as if I'd known them my whole life. And while they made my life sound like a dream, there was one thing they didn't know.

The man I wanted didn't want me. At least his excuse —which was a really good excuse—was that dealing with a student in any romantic way would kill his career.

"I can assure you, Penelope, nothing you or anyone else does can ruin me."

I bit my bottom lip, feeling the sudden urge to take a drive, but I'd wait until tomorrow when I returned to campus.

Then, I wouldn't take my eyes off Professor Lucas.

5

Penelope

I breathed in the salty smell of the New York streets, mingling with the scent of freshly-cut grass from the school's fields as watched Dominic walk out of the campus gates, his tall and muscular figure a sight to behold. He wore a navy-blue suit that hugged his broad shoulders and a crisp white shirt accentuating his chiseled jawline. His dark hair was neatly combed to the side, and a pair of aviator sunglasses shielded his eyes from the bright sun.

As he walked, my eyes were stuck on his gait—confident and purposeful, each step solid and steady. The wind picked up, causing his tie to gently flap in the breeze. I couldn't help but admire the way he moved, the way he carried himself.

I wondered what kind of man he was, what his life was like outside the school's walls. I'd convinced myself that was the reason I was following him—to find out what he did on his own time, when he wasn't advising students.

Dominic slipped inside a beautiful red vintage Convertible, and I hurried to slide into my sleek silver Infiniti, following behind him at a safe distance. I admired the car for a moment, taking in its curves and lines, before turning my attention back to Dominic.

The road wound its way through the outskirts of town, the sun slowly dipping below the horizon, casting a golden glow over everything. I rolled down my car windows, and the wind blew my hair in all directions. I caught a whiff of the sweet aroma of freshly baked bread coming from a nearby bakery, mixing with the cool winds.

As Dominic turned into a quiet suburban street, I followed him, my heart beating faster with anticipation. But to my dismay, a security gate blocked my access to his home. I parked my car off to the side and waited, hoping he would come back out.

Hours passed, and I sat in my car, my mind wandering. I couldn't help but remember the kiss we shared two nights before. It had been unexpected, but it felt like magic. The way his lips moved against mine and his hands held me tightly left a lasting impression on me. I couldn't get him out of my head, and now I was becoming a stalker.

"I'm really losing it."

I checked my rearview mirror, lifted my cell, and wished I had his number.

What would I say?

I had no idea. I couldn't explain why I was so drawn to him. It wasn't as if I'd never kissed a man before. But there was something intensely intriguing about Dominic that I couldn't let go of. Something that drew me to him and made me want to stay forever.

I sighed. "Now you sound like Sofia." I groaned. Not that being in like with a guy was a bad thing, but to the point of stalking, sure, sure.

My cell buzzed, and I lifted it and answered it without looking at the caller ID.

"You've reached me."

Emma laughed. "Good. You know. We were all so busy catching up yesterday that I forgot to ask you something. When Alice, Sofia, and I returned from the bathroom the night before, you were gone."

I smirked.

"Where'd you go?"

"Outside."

"Why?"

"For some fresh air."

The line became quiet, and I looked at the phone to see if she was still there.

"Hmmm. Why do I get the feeling you're leaving something out?"

"What is there to leave out?"

"This is what you're supposed to be telling me."

"Oh, you know what. There is a thing. The guy I'd been dancing with most of the night thought I was supposed to go home with him because he'd supplied the drinks."

"Oh, no..."

"Yeah. I'm truly stunned that some men still believe you owe them pussy for drinks." I huffed. "As if."

"Right. So what did you say?"

"He got rough with me, and I slapped him."

Emma gasped.

"I sure did. And he was about to hit me back until this guy intervened."

"Guy?"

"Yes. A handsome guy at that."

"What! Now you know you were supposed to let us know this."

"Like you said, we were busy chatting and catching up on other things."

"What happened after that?"

"I thanked him, and he left just as quickly as he appeared."

"And you just let him?"

"Of course not. That's why I was gone when you all came out of the ladies' room."

"Ooooh, now we're getting to the truth of the matter."

I laughed. "I did want to get some air, too."

"Mm-hmm. Then what happened?"

Our line quieted as my thoughts ventured back to our standdown, the way his hands gripped my thighs, and our mouths crashed. I shivered.

"Well?"

"Nothing. The man was in a hurry, and he...got away."

I could admit I lied because I wanted Dominic all to myself, in every aspect. After all, I didn't want to jeopardize his job, even if he said he couldn't be ruined. A part of me wanted to show him I could be trustworthy. So, I made it my business to keep whatever we were doing on the hush.

"Are you lying to me?"

I smirked but kept my voice neutral. "Now why would I be lying?"

"You're smart enough to know I could get the video pulled from the club if I wanted to."

I laughed and shook my head. "Using your father's power to call my bluff is a threat. Are you threatening me, friend?"

"Yes."

I laughed louder and she held her stance.

"Fine. Call your father—or better yet, throw his name around to get what you want. Just remember, if you're wrong, you have to fix me a full five-course meal for your lack of trust."

"What?!"

"You heard me."

"And you know I can't cook."

"I want a full five-course meal, complete with desserts baked right from the oven by your hands."

"And what happens if I can't give you that?"

"Then I get to take your cell phone for a month. No communications with anyone, including that jock you're wanting to seduce."

She gasped again. "That is so not fair!"

"Hmm...imagine how I feel when you tell me you're throwing around your father's power to get what you think you're not getting out of me. Doesn't seem quite fair, does it?"

Emma sucked in a deep breath. "You sure are going through great lengths to keep this covered."

I snickered. "Emma, you've never accused me of lying to you like this. I don't understand where this is coming from."

"You told me you stepped outside to get some air; then suddenly there's a whole story about a sexy guy who saved you. Forgive me if I only half-believe you just let him get away."

"What would be the difference if I didn't?"

"See! I knew it!"

I pursed my lips. "Emma, please calm down. The guy didn't want anything to do with me. If you don't believe me, pull the tapes; you'll see he got away."

Which was true. Dominic had stepped out of the elevator and left me panting as the doors closed. My pussy thumped just thinking about it.

The line quieted, and then Emma sighed. "I guess. I won't push it. If and when you run into this mystery guy again, I better be the first to know about it."

"Okay. Don't get your panties in a bunch."

"What are you doing now?"

The gates to Corniquea Hills opened and a motor-cycle revved and flew out before the gates could fully open. On the seat, bent forward, clutching the handles with gloved hands, sat Dominic.

His gorgeousness hit me like a ton of bricks. In the absence of a jacket, a white sleeveless T-shirt stretched across his chiseled torso. Destroyed denim jeans rode his thighs, combat boots on his feet, aviator glasses across his eyes.

I sucked in a breath and was so caught up in his striking appearance that I almost forgot to put the car in drive to follow him.

"Hello? Hello?" Emma shouted.

"Emma, I'll call you back in a minute." I disconnected the call before Emma could respond and hit the gas. At the light I made a quick U-turn and rushed to catch up with him, but Dominic zigzagged through access points I couldn't reach.

"Come on, come on!" I shouted, half-frustrated with Dominic's highway antics while admiring them all the same.

"Why does this man turn me on so much?"

That was something I was still trying to figure out. Cars honked as I swerved in front of them. "Sorry!"

Middle fingers were produced from some drivers

while others shouted at me, outraged by my reckless driving.

"Where exactly are you going, Professor Lucas?" I murmured, keeping my eyes on him from four cars behind.

Traffic slowed, but Dominic crossed an intersection when the light turned yellow and the car in front of me slowed to a stop.

"No! No! Noooo! Come on!"

Quickly, I stomped my accelerator, pulled around the car and shot through the intersection just as the traffic in the opposite direction also moved.

Horns blew and I grimaced. My eyes jumped from the rearview to the road in front of me. The sky was shifting to a dark gray as the nightlife of the city awakened.

"Burlesque Boulevard?" I frowned. "Now why would he be going there?"

Burlesque Boulevard was home to sex workers. Johns escaped being detained during certain hours of the day when the police were busy in other high-traffic areas and they took advantage of those perks.

Dominic made a left turn, but flashing red and blue lights behind me drew my attention.

"Shit."

I sighed and pulled over to the side of the road and put the car in park. But even as I waited for the officer to approach, my eyes never left the entrance of the street Dominic had ridden down.

Knock, knock, knock!

I pursed my lips and rolled the window down. The officer bent forward and stared at me.

"Are you in a rush to get somewhere?"

"I'm not now."

He frowned. "License and registration."

I reached into the glove compartment and removed the registration, then dug into my Kate Spade purse, and offered my license.

"Wait here."

He left and I rolled the window back up and blew out a harsh breath. "So good for staying out of trouble, Penelope," I muttered.

Twenty minutes passed and I grew impatient. I glanced in the rearview to see the officer reapproaching. "Finally," I whispered.

He handed me a yellow ticket. "Slow down, or next time, go to jail."

I nodded. "It won't happen again."

"Good."

He peered at me, and then left after turning off his lights. As soon as he pulled off so did I, turning left on the street Dominic had ventured down.

6

Penelope

I immediately regretted following him. Burlesque Boulevard was crowded with women in scanty, suggestive clothing; on the sidewalk, in the street, on balconies, whistling and catcalling.

That, however, wasn't what freaked me out. The men scattered around, slavered over the women at every turn. It was like they were in a candy shop wanting to taste-test everything in sight.

I sighed.

There was no sign of Dominic; I shouldn't have been surprised. My car moved five miles per hour as I maneuvered through the crowd, trying not to run anyone over.

Curious eyes turned my way, and a group of men strolled in front of my fender, causing me to press the brakes.

They stared at me, and I stared back.

"You might be in the wrong part of town, honey," a lady from my left shouted. I glanced at her, then back at the boys, and blew my horn.

Another mistake.

The sound only brought more attention my way, and soon, my Infiniti was surrounded.

There was not much that scared me—except thunderstorms and phone calls in the middle of the night. But I could admit that a bit of fear crept into my soul when my view was blocked entirely.

I was unsure how to react. Should I call the police, call somebody, anybody? Should I scream at them, blow the horn again?

While I went through possible options and scenarios, my door was yanked open.

"Hey, what the hell!" I grabbed the handle and yanked it back. But it was forced open. I tried hitting the gas pedal but was dragged from the seat. Simultaneously, I wished a few things—that I'd worn my seat belt, minded my business, and locked my car doors. But it was too late for that now.

"Get off me! Are you crazy? What the hell!"

I pushed and shouted and slapped one guy while another gripped my arm and yanked me from him. My car revved when I noticed someone else was behind the wheel. The crowd moved for them, and they took off, stealing it right before my eyes. I shoved and pushed as I was pulled and groped.

"Heeeeelp!" I fought with all my might. "Heeeeelp!"

"Come on, leave her alone," shouted that same woman who'd told me I was in the wrong part of town.

They ignored her. I pushed one away as another grabbed me. Every time I fought one, grips came from others.

Boos chorused from the women as they showed their disagreement with what was happening to me. Still, I couldn't help but notice *they* were left untouched. Neither did they move to help me get away.

Seconds felt like minutes when suddenly I was released.

I whipped around, quickly becoming dizzy when I saw one of the guys who'd gripped me go flying over the boulevard. Where he had stood, another guy was on the ground howling in pain while others backed away in a rush.

I blinked, sucked in a breath, steadied myself, and yelped when another hand touched my back. Twirling on my heels, my eyes met Dominic's dark, heavy-lidded gaze.

"Oh my God!"

I threw myself around his muscular frame, trembling as I gripped him like my life depended on it.

He hesitated initially, but then his arms embraced me, scooping me up, allowing me to lock my body around his.

We were moving then. I didn't know where we were going, but I didn't care. I was safe. For the time I was in his arms, I was safe. My racing heart leveled out, along with the dizziness that once took hold of me. It was then that I noticed four men following us. They didn't look like the johns—more like security dressed in black. A closer look and they were obviously Italian, silent, and moving in sync.

I gripped Dominic tighter. He was the only one I trusted.

His footsteps paused.

"*Apri quella dannata porta,*" he said. I recognized the language as Italian, and the dark timbre of his voice caused heat to spill down my skin. It was the first time I'd heard Dominic speak the language, and I watched the men rush to open the door in front of us.

I glanced at them again, curious as to who they were. We moved inside a building, and a sweet and spicy incense hit my nose. Pool tables were stationed around, and smoke from cigars filtered through the air. Men were drinking, a few women were scattered about, and an atmosphere of calmness was carried through the space.

It was a billiard club.

I frowned. *Is that where he'd gone? To a billiard club?*

We turned down a corridor, and one of the men hurried to open another door so we could enter.

Inside, a medium-sized section cut off from the main area was empty except for a bartender, stationed behind a long, polished bar on the left side of the room. Three small raised stages with strip poles were stationed in the middle of the floor. Lounge furniture, made of the most expensive leather in shades of white decorated the space.

"Leave us."

The men disappeared, and for the first time, Dominic and I eyed each other. A flash of our kiss in that elevator bombarded me as my eyes crept over his hard, chiseled face down to his lips.

The spicy aphrodisiac that cruised from him wasn't his cologne alone. I knew his scent—had smelled it in his office when he'd stuck his tongue in my mouth, in the library when I'd collided with his chest, in the elevator when he'd pinned me to the walls, and now, it teased me as my chest rose and fell against his.

Gray eyes stared at me, filled with concern. But as quickly as I saw that concern, it changed to a glare.

Dominic peeled me away from his body and plopped me down on the sofa, annoyance changing his handsome features into a rugged, frustrated menace.

"What the fuck are you doing here?"

I sucked in a breath. "Where is here, exactly?"

"Penelope."

Hearing my name drop from his mouth sent a shiver straight to my pussy.

"I..." I sighed.

"You were following me."

"Is that a question or...?"

His glare intensified.

"I can tell you right now, that look you're doing...

although it shows you're not pleased, I'd rather be confronted with it any day than what just happened to me back there so you can't get rid of me with it."

He sighed, the concern fighting its way back to the surface of his face. "You shouldn't have come here."

"Where is here, if you don't mind me asking?"

"Why would you follow me? What is it about me that has your curiosity so piqued?"

"Everything."

He gritted his teeth. "You're in danger."

My eyes widened, and an involuntary shutter slipped down my flesh. "What is that supposed to mean?"

"Every time you do something because of your curiosity, it puts you in danger, Penelope."

"How?"

"Do you really need to ask that question?"

"Yes!"

"What just happened to you?"

"I..." My mind shuffled, and I grimaced. "I'm not sure."

"You're not sure?"

"I was assaulted."

"What else?"

I swallowed, frustrated that he made me relive what happened when all I wanted to do was get away from it.

"What else, Penelope?"

I released an exasperated breath. "My car was stolen."

His glare was back, but his voice remained steady.

"Go on."

"I'm confused. What the hell is going on here? Those men back there didn't touch the other women unless the women gave them permission," I mumbled. "Though they looked like prey circling their meals," I shuddered. "But they were quick to assault me. What the hell was that?"

"Would you rather they assault them, too?"

"No!" He stared at me, and my frustration grew. "Of course not! I just don't understand why they bullied me?"

"You're an outsider, Penelope. You should've never come here. Those women are protected. The regulars know that. They have no morals or empathy, and if I would not have heard you scream, they would've—"

"Please don't say it!"

He paused, gritting his teeth again. "You need to hear it."

My eyes widened. "Why?"

"It's clear you've been sheltered your entire life. This... my life," he paused, correcting himself, careful about what to share. "You don't belong here. There is nothing interesting about me."

"I beg to differ."

He exhaled harshly. "Got damn it, Penelope."

Every time my name shot from his mouth, my pussy thumped, and it was then I realized there was a craving buried deep inside me that wanted to come out. I wanted to sit my pussy on that mouth of his—wanted to ride his face in a backward-cowgirl position where he could suck my clit and lick my ass simultaneously.

An unintentional moan slipped from my lips, and the sound shocked me. My nipples hardened, and heat teased my flesh. I bit down on my lip as Dominic squinted at me.

I rushed to speak again. "Furthermore, I'm not this sheltered little princess like you think. Hell, my parents are practically Bonnie and Clyde."

This seemed to pique his interest as his brows rose, and he cocked his head to the side. "Is that right?"

"Well...they were. But anyway, the point is, I've seen things and heard bad things."

"Bad?"

"Yeah."

He nodded. "Have you ever experienced any of these bad things, Penelope?"

I crossed my legs and tightened them in an effort to keep my pussy from throbbing.

"No."

"So technically, it's like you've read a book or watched a television show?"

I frowned and pursed my lips. "Well—"

"You don't belong here!"

I jerked back, his outburst shocking me, though it shouldn't have.

"Boss." A man peeked his head in the door, and Dominic turned his glare on him. "I apologize. I didn't know you had company."

"Speak!" Dominic shouted.

"You have a phone call. It's important."

Dominic's eyebrow twitched and he turned back to me but didn't say another word. A whistle rang from his lips, and a server approached.

"Give her whatever she wants."

"Yes, sir."

He glared at me once more, then left the room.

"Miss, would you like something to drink or eat?"

I nodded absently, my mind stuck on the fact that that man had called Dominic *boss*. Now, I was more curious than ever.

"Yes," I said.

The server nodded as he handed me a folder. "This is our menu if you'd like to review it and tell me what you desire."

I glanced down at the menu, mindlessly looking over the options. "Chicken wings, fries, tequila with lime, water." I handed the menu back.

"I'll be back with your drinks. Your food will be prepared fresh, so give it about twenty minutes."

"Thank you." He moved to scurry off.

"Hey..." He turned back. "Can I ask you a question?"

"Sure."

"What's the name of this place?"

He frowned but quickly answered me. "The Lu Billiards Club."

My eyes widened. "This is Dameon Lucas's club?"

"Yes, miss."

"Oh....does Dominic work here?"

He frowned. "I'm sorry?"

"I just noticed the guy called him boss, so I assumed he works here."

"Um...well, you must ask Dominic about his roles."

"I mean, is he the boss, or isn't he?"

"He's definitely the boss."

I nodded. "Okay. So that settles it. Wow. Amazing that he could work full-time at the school and run a billiards club. He's the jack of all trades, it seems."

The server peered at me, then nodded. "Yes, well, will there be anything else?"

"If I have more questions, I'll let you know."

He nodded and rushed off. If I didn't know better, I'd think he didn't want to answer more of my questions.

I wondered if everyone was as secretive as Dominic. Rising to my feet, I strolled to a window at the back of the room. Peeking out, I saw some of the same men who'd assaulted me, drinking and slipping money into the bras of some of the women.

"This is the wild, wild west," I murmured. Annoyance crept over me when I thought of my Infiniti. I could call and report it stolen, but unfortunately, my cell phone, purse, credit cards, and license were in my car. "Shit!"

I turned and left the room in a hurry, going in search of a telephone.

7

Dominic

"I've found him. I'll bring him to you."

"That's my boy. I knew I could depend on you to hunt Gianni down."

"I haven't been a boy for a long time, Father."

He paused, coughed, cleared his throat, and mumbled through the line. "Yes, yes. Perhaps I should make you my right hand. I need someone who can get things done around here."

"Dameon—"

"Shut the fuck up, Rolando."

I smirked. I could see Rolando's smug face in the background, staring at Dameon in disbelief.

"When you leave there, bring him to me."

"I'll be there soon."

The line dropped, and I sat the phone in its cradle and left the office, strolling back to the lounge. When I entered, it was empty, and a full plate of food sat untouched on the table. I inhaled a deep breath and went in search of Penelope.

She ground my gears, and it annoyed me that she'd been able to follow me without me spotting her.

Never had I let anyone tail me without spotting them. How the hell did she? As much as I wanted an answer, it wasn't the most important thing. I'd learned a lesson. I wasn't without mistakes.

I told Dameon no woman could infiltrate my world, but I'd somehow let Penelope inch her way in. Though she was at the entrance, that was close enough, too close, but getting rid of her seemed to be the biggest challenge of my life—mostly because she wouldn't go, but also because I wanted her to stay.

I found her at the bar arguing with Mano, my capo. I frowned; my face twisted in displeasure when I approached.

"What the fuck seems to be the problem?"

She whipped around and reached for me, her hands gripping my torso as she stepped close. "This man won't let me use the phone. It's ridiculous!"

I removed her hands because her touch did odd things to my libido, and I didn't need to think about shoving my dick inside her right now. "Who do you need to call?"

Her brows dipped, and I adored the pout that pushed her lips out.

"My car was stolen. Everything is in it. All my

personal belongings. As far as I know, my credit cards are being maxed out, and my bank account is depleted!"

"Lower your voice."

She went to respond but closed her lips. Her obedience aroused me, and I caught myself staring at her mouth.

"So, who do you plan to call?"

Confusion settled across her face. "The police, hello?"

"No."

Her eyes widened. "No? What do you mean, no?"

"Don't make me repeat myself, Penelope."

She swallowed the words on her tongue, and her legs crossed. My brows rose as I assessed her body language. She was aroused by me calling her name. That wouldn't be good for either of us if I were correct.

"I need to—"

"Your car will be returned. Whatever was stolen from your accounts will be replaced. Anything else?"

Her eyes widened again, and she glanced at Mano, who held a smirk, then back at me. "Can I talk to you in private?"

"Your food is waiting for you back in the lounge."

She took a step forward, then hesitated and glanced over her shoulder to make sure I was there.

"Proceed."

Her eyes slipped up my torso to meet my gaze, and then she continued walking.

Back in the lounge, she sat on the couch, said a quick prayer, and dug into her food. While she ate, everything was quiet in the room. One thing about Penelope; she was full of words, primarily questions—which irritated me—but words, nonetheless.

Her tongue slipped from her mouth as she indulged in the food, but it was such a significant portion of food the kitchen offered that she barely made it through before sitting back, full.

"Those are the best wings I've ever tasted. Shit. Who's in the kitchen—Gordan Ramsey?" She laughed at her joke, lifted her glass of tequila, and took a sip.

"Have you eaten?"

"No."

"You should have some of this. I'm not going to eat it all."

"I'm not hungry." Just then, my stomach growled, loud and ravenous, like an untamed animal lived inside me.

Penelope's mouth opened in a gasp. "I think you're starving."

"Yes, but not for food."

Her eyes dropped to my lips. "What are you hungry for, Dominic?"

Her voice had dropped an octave, and my dick jumped with the rise in my pulse.

"I need to take you home."

"So you can eat?"

My dick jumped again, and it was taking all my might not to grab her throat and fuck her relentlessly on the couch.

"Are we talking about food, Penelope?"

Her hand slipped down her jeans between her thighs. "I'm not."

"Give me your address."

She rattled it off quickly as if she'd been waiting for me to ask.

I turned from her, stood to my feet, and strolled to the door.

"Let's go."

SHE HELD me tight as we navigated the dark streets on my bike.

"Woooooo hoooo!"

I smirked. Penelope sounded like a college student on a night out with her boyfriend. I wondered if she ever had any real fun. But then, my kind of fun wasn't most people's. It would likely scare her heart right out of her chest.

I picked up speed, zipping around cars, in and out of traffic, speeding down side streets, cutting up one-ways to get to her side of town.

Lights flickered past us in a blink, the wind at our backs, and the rules of the road forgotten as I drove.

"You are crazy!" she shouted.

I revved the engine, and we got up to one hundred and twenty miles per hour.

"This can't be safe!"

I revved the engine again, and she held me so tight I knew she was terrified.

"Please slow down!"

I crossed an intersection when the light turned red, and police sirens pulled behind us. My speed increased, and I blew through two additional intersections, cut down an alley, and shot onto the interstate, leaving the cops in the wind.

"You're going to give me a heart attack!" Penelope shouted.

I laughed and her fear supercharged my heartbeat.

"Calm down!" I shouted into the wind, but she only tightened her grip and buried her face in my back.

I was trying to avoid the hospital at all costs. I whipped around a big rig and made it across town in no time.

As soon as I slowed, so did the beat of her heart, but when I pulled into her driveway, she jumped off my bike and rushed onto the front porch of the contemporary stucco home.

Dark laughter surfed from my gut. "Why are you running?" I teased. "Devil on your heels?"

She fumbled with the keys to her entrance. "You're crazy as hell."

Penelope was flustered, and I was amused. "I keep trying to tell you that, and you don't seem to understand it."

She twirled around, her eyes wide, and her finger

pointed at me. "Is that what this was all about? Showing me how crazy you are?" She poked me in the chest as I met up with her on the porch. I smirked.

"You haven't seen my crazy, Penelope. Trust me."

She stared, and for a long minute, she contemplated what I meant.

"Whatever." She turned from me and entered the house.

Thunder crackled in the clouds, and lightning streaked across the heavens.

"Remember," I said, turning to leave. "Don't call the police. If you do, never mention me. Do you understand, Penelope?"

"Where are you going?"

I paused, turned an inquiring gaze back at her, and the first thing I noticed was her hand against the doorframe, trembling.

I faced her. "I'm leaving."

"I thought we were coming here to...you know."

"To what?"

"So you could eat, and we could...."

I waited for her to continue, and another roar of thunder raged through the sky.

"Please don't leave."

This woman, with whom I had no business with outside of regular campus hours, made me act out of my norms. And nothing I did to deter her, did.

"I can get food anywhere, Penelope. I can't stay here with you."

"Why? I'm an adult, so spare me the student-teacher bullshit."

"That's a nasty mouth you got there, Penelope. I didn't take you for a filthy girl."

"That's because you won't stay around me long enough to find out."

My dick was at it again, pulsing against my pants, wanting to be freed.

I sucked in a breath, turned my back, and went to my bike, throwing my leg over and adjusting my helmet.

Another round of thunder crackled, and she dropped her keys and ran into the house, leaving the door ajar. I frowned, hesitated, and locked my jaw.

"Go, Lucas," I chanted to myself. "Get the fuck out of here."

Still, I hesitated, watching the entrance to her home while willing myself to leave.

I glanced down her street. Penelope's neighborhood was quiet; it was a suburban population located in an upscale part of New York. It was apparent that she was wealthy which made me wonder about her family's background.

A loud crash inside her home made me dismount from the bike.

"Fuck."

I climbed the porch and entered, crossing the foyer

and slamming the door behind me. My eyes carried over high tray ceilings, mirrors that lined the walls, and vivid yellow and orange colors splashed throughout her decor.

It was easy to find her. She'd turned on a light in every room she entered, creating a path to her bedroom.

I paused at the entrance and glanced around the large space to the canopy bed, where she covered herself with a duvet.

Frowning, I entered slowly, crossing the room to a window to inspect the neighborhood again. It was a habit of mine.

Technically, Dameon had ordered me to stick with bodyguards at all times. The Lucas Cosa Nostra was not without enemies. But he knew I was a lone wolf. Therefore, I kept my guard high and always assessed wherever I found myself.

"What is with you and thunderstorms?" I asked. I turned my attention her way when she yanked the cover off her face.

"I thought you were leaving?"

I sighed. I hated repeating myself, and if Penelope had been paying attention, she would know this by now.

She licked her lips. "It's a ridiculous story I don't want to recount."

Thunder made her jump back underneath the cover.

"Are you going to be okay when I leave?"

"No."

My nostrils flared. "What do you normally do when there's a thunderstorm?"

"Turn on all the lights, turn up the stereo, and stand in the kitchen with a knife in my hand."

I frowned. "Someone hurt you."

She pulled the cover from her face and stared at me.

"Who was it?"

She didn't respond and the silence stretched until thunder crackled again.

"Come closer, Dominic."

I gritted my teeth, glanced out her window to check her street again, crouched, unlaced my boots, and stepped out of them.

At the side of her bed, Penelope drew the covers back, revealing a perfectly lean body, butterscotch skin with a perfect curve at her hips. I sucked in a breath; she'd taken her clothes off sometime between running into the house and climbing into bed but left her black lace thong and bra on to tease me.

"Penelope..." I growled.

"Are you going to stand there watching, or are you still hungry, professor?"

I locked my jaw and grabbed her ankles, pulling her to the edge of the bed. On my knees, I sank my face into her belly, inhaling the scent of her flesh, my eyes closed as a wicked snarl moved through me. Penelope had no idea how much trouble she was in, but remaining on this path, she would find out.

I bit into her stomach, my teeth piercing her flesh, and she shuddered, releasing a light yelp.

"Dominic..." she whispered.

I yanked the string to her thong, ripping it apart and yanked the pieces from her body. Light brown curly hair lightly swept across her pussy, a light peach fragrance I couldn't put my finger on drifting from her essence.

"You don't fuckin' listen," I growled, stuffing my face between the apex of her thighs. "I told you to leave. Then I tried to leave. But no... you just don't fuckin' listen, Penelope."

I felt her shiver as the heat from my mouth tickled her flesh. I tossed her thighs over my shoulders and covered her pussy with the stretch of my tongue. Sucking, I closed my eyes, indulged in the sweet, light peach taste that filled my mouth as her hips bucked and she hissed.

A moan drifted from my gut, but it sounded more like a snarl. My entire body lit up, chills sweeping across me as if I'd connected with a source that ignited my central nervous system. I suddenly felt stronger, wilder, more untamed as I sucked her full pussy, then tongued her clit as if it were her mouth. The pleasure that ripped through me tingled my ears and the soles of my feet and stretched my dick to the point that it ached.

"Fuck."

Her body twitched, her hips bouncing against my mouth, riding the sensation of pleasure I gave on her back.

"Aaaaaah! Oooooh.... Dominic, yes!"

Her desire filled my ears, accelerating the pleasure I gave because I wanted to hear more.

"Sssssssssss!"

Hips bucking, her hands slipped across my head and gripped the sides. Her head fell back, mouth open, purrs drifting from her throat as her hips bucked.

She trembled and twitched, moaned, and purred, pumped her hips and threw her wet flesh at me like a bouncing yoyo. I devoured her, lulled into her spellbound allure, captivated by the way her essence ignited every atom in my soul. I couldn't stop. My tongue swept across her pussy, dug inside her entrance, and tongued her clit as I gripped her thighs and pulled her tighter.

I sucked and slurped and pampered her pussy with light and heavy strokes from my tongue.

"Shiiiiiiiit! Dominic..." She lost her breath. "I'm cumming, aaaaaaaaaah!"

I lost myself in her flavor, striking her clit and driving my tongue inside her again. "Mmmmmmm," I moaned, struck by the taste of her orgasm.

"Shit! Shit!" Her body twitched, her pulse whacking hard, the pulsation between her thighs fighting back against my tongue.

"Dominic!"

I teased her by sucking her harder, which I knew would drive her crazy since she'd released a powerful ass nut.

"Pleaaaaase, ah!"

I pulled back and bit her inside thigh. She yelped, and I turned to bite the other. I wanted more of her in my mouth. I wasn't done eating. But I guess this would have to do.

With the way she moved, shoving her hips away from me while holding onto my face, I assumed she wanted me to move while simultaneously wanting me to stay.

"You can't have it both ways, goddess."

A moan slipped from her lips as she pulled me forward. I lifted and drifted, hovering over her heavy lids as she looked up at me.

"Fuck me, Dominic."

I gritted my teeth. "I have to go."

"No, you can't leave me like this."

"You mean light and airy after a powerful nut?"

She laughed, the melodic sound music to my ears.

"You're right. This is the best way to be left."

I smirked, dropped my lips onto her mouth, stole her breath, gave her back her flavor, and then left. And by the time she'd realized I was gone, Penelope was most likely fast asleep.

8

Dominic

Forty minutes.

That's how long it took me to do what I need to after leaving Penelope's home.

I stopped at the warehouse where I housed my death gear—chains, saws, hatchets, knives, guns—which I used only as a last resort. Guns could be traced. Not mine, but still, they were risky. I changed clothes, boots, added a ski mask to cover my face and gloves, and grabbed a baseball bat. I checked the monitor I had set up to view Rolando's mansion.

As expected, he wasn't there, and the capos that watched his building were huddled together, puffing on cigars.

Those motherfuckers were good for nothing, and that's how I was able to slip onto the compound unseen, drag Gianni from a shed in the back, and knock him over the head to keep him asleep until we arrived here, at Dameon's.

BEFORE WE ENTERED, I pulled to the side of the road, switched my gear again, dumping what I had on in a black duffle bag in the trunk.

I rolled the window down on the Range Rover as I pulled to the gate. A capo approached. "Need help with something?"

"Someone get this motherfucker out of my trunk."

I popped the opener and watched them in the rearview pull Gianni out of the trunk.

Back at my side, the capo spoke again. "You need your car detailed?"

"What the fuck do you think?"

He nodded. "When you park, I'll grabbed the others and take care of it."

"And don't touch my luggage."

"Of course not."

I glared at him, drove inside, parked, and met Dameon at the side entrance.

Capos walked forward, dragging Gianni but holding him upright. Gianni, slumped over, still slept from my bat's beating.

"Look at this son of a bitch," Dameon barked. He slapped Rolando on the shoulder and ordered, "Wake 'em up!"

Rolando barked orders in our native tongue, and a capo stepped forward and slipped smelling salts underneath his nose.

Gianni's body jerked backward, his eyes popping open like a wild animal as he quickly glanced around.

"Ooooooooou!" he howled as pain from his concussion hit him like a mountain of bricks. He pulled from the capos and balled up into a fetal position on the ground.

"Get 'em up!" Saliva flew from Dameon's mouth. He was pissed, and I was amused.

"Ouuuuuu! Ouuuuu!"

"Shut the fuck up, you imbecile!" Dameon kicked Gianni three times, and he continued to howl in pain.

"You might have to give him a minute. He's obviously in no position to focus on your questions."

Dameon turned his frustration to Rolando. "And why is that, I wonder!?"

"The sooner we get him some help, the sooner we can get answers from him."

Frustration seeped from Dameon. His brows dipped and eyes were wild as he burned with fury. His gaze turned to me, and I gave him back the riddled frustration masking my face.

"Where did you find this motherfucker?"

"In a ditch two miles from Rolando's."

His eyes widened, as did Rolando's.

"Bullshit!" Rolando spat. "No one can get that close to my compound without being spotted!"

I ignored him, which he hated, and spoke to Dameon. "Father, it's as simple as checking the security footage, which I have already done, but if you'd like to go behind me, you're within your right to do so."

Dameon stared at me for a long moment, then squinted at Rolando. When his eyes shifted back to me, he cleared his throat.

"I don't know what's happening between you two, but I need you to fix it. You're my son, and I love you more than life itself." He glanced at Rolando. "You're the eyes behind my head. If your compound can be breached, then so can mine, and that is a big fuckin' problem."

"Dameon, you know I keep security tight. No one can breach either of our estates unless it's him!"

He pointed at me, eyes wide and accusatory. I'd been waiting for this moment. I knew it was bound to come eventually, but I didn't see it happening this soon.

"So then, I'm the Black Rose, is that it, Rolando?"

Dameon's words tumbled out of his mouth in an Italian rush.

"Rolando, don't force me to cut your fucking tongue out and feed it to the dogs motherfucker!"

Rolando's eyes grew, and I only stared at him, teasing him with a light smirk that was barely noticeable but got my point across.

Rolando exhaled sharply, turned his back, and then faced us again. He knew this was a game he couldn't win.

It angered him to his core that I was the only person who could get in Dameon's ear over him.

"Maybe I should go to Italy. Let you...fix things here while I assist Bruno with operations there."

Dameon continued his outburst in Italian.

"You will do no such fuckin' thing! You're to stay by my side! Bruno has everything under control there. We need control here! I don't give a motherfuck what Rolando says!"

I responded to him the same.

"I can't deal with your jealous consigliere. *He's been barking at me for a while now, and I've let it slide for you, Father. But insinuating I had anything to do with Gianni's disappearance is calling me a traitor, and I don't take lightly to that. He's only still breathing at this moment because of you. I must leave."*

I turned my back and took a few steps.

"Dominic!"

I paused, held back my laugh, and faced him with the same mask of fury reminiscent on his face.

"You will stay." Silence filled our space, then: *"Rolando will go."*

"What?!" Rolando screamed, incensed. *"I will do no such thing!"*

Dameon's brows dipped. *"You will if I say you will."*

I stepped in. *"Let him stay. There are problems only he can fix."* I pulled out a phone, tapped the screen, and held it toward Dameon. Rolando eased closer to view the video and witness his capos—smoking and seemingly distracted from their duties.

A flagrant rise of expletives dropped from Dameon's mouth.

"I will visit Bruno to ensure he doesn't need my assistance. While I'm away, Rolando will fix what is broken and prove that he deserves to stay."

I eyed Rolando, and he glared at me, but I'd just done him a favor while looking out for my own best interest. The trip to Italy wasn't because I wanted to give Rolando another chance but rather to get closer to the next mark on my list. Rolando had just opened the door to give me an excuse to take the jet, and I didn't have to watch him to make sure his eyes weren't on me.

He had a task now; to show his strength in the Lucas Cosa Nostra and prove to his boss that he was worthy of the position. It was perfect, and I was so pleased that I needed to bust a nut.

My thoughts shifted to Penelope. I inhaled a deep breath, and her scent, still on my mouth, filled my nostrils. I licked my lips and retasted her, as I considered going back to her home and fuckin' her persistently.

But the recourse I needed now would surely split her forcefully if I stuck my cock in her, and I had to question myself: why did I care?

Usually, when I wanted or needed something, I got it. No one said no to me, even if they were harmed in the process. But now, for some odd fuckin' reason, I wanted

Penelope to experience only pleasure from me. Yet, I also would like that pleasure to accompany pain. It's what drove my engine.

I was fuckin' twisted. I took no responsibility and blamed Dameon for the growth of the twisted corridors of my soul.

This was what life handed me. And I played the cards I was dealt.

"ONE WEEK," Dameon said. *"And you come back here. Meet me for dinner. You and me only."*

"Yes, Father."

I left without glancing at Rolando. But I knew his anger had reached a boiling point.

9

Penelope

Light conversation filled the classroom as we waited for the professor to arrive. I checked my watch and glanced around, but my mind remained with Dominic. After he left me sprawled on the bed soaking wet, I crawled under the cover and fell asleep without putting up a fight about him leaving.

This morning while brushing my teeth, I imagined the bristles on the toothbrush nibbles from his mouth and almost tongued my toothbrush. A smile curved my lips, and I dropped my head to hide my blush.

Emma, Alice, and Sofia, slid into adjacent seats.

"Since none of you have asked, I should tell you I took your advice."

Simultaneously, Emma, Alice, and I looked at Sofia.

"Which was?" Emma asked.

"I've been ignoring Ethan. He's tried to get my attention at every turn, and I've shoved him off. I can tell it hurt his feelings, by the way."

"I don't remember advising you to ignore him," I said.

Her eyes widened, and she shrieked, "What?"

"Neither did I," Emma added. Alice nodded in agreement, and we all stared back at Sofia.

"Am I living in the twilight zone? Are you doppelgangers?"

"She's so dramatic," I whispered to Emma.

"Most of the time," Emma agreed.

"Hey!"

We smirked and glanced at each other, then burst into laughter. Curious eyes turned our way as other classmates wondered what was so funny.

"You guys, that is not funny!"

"Oh, come on, Sofia, you know we have to have a little fun."

"At my expense?"

"Technically, we didn't tell you to ignore him," Emma added.

"We told you to not give up the goods to him. The two are not interchangeable."

"Well, call me silly, but I can't be nice and indulge in conversation without falling in love with him, okay?"

Alice's face drew up in a frown. "So that means you've got to ignore and be mean?"

"Yes," Sofia said, as if it were common sense.

Emma shook her head. "You poor doll. I hate that for you."

Alice nodded as Sofia dropped her face in the palms of her hands.

"Ugh! I've got to find someone else to like. I don't know how long I'll be able to ignore Ethan before I give in."

"Trust me," I said, "it's better this way."

She dropped her hands, her eyebrows going in different directions when she responded. "How? Please enlighten me."

"Because if you give in and give up the goods, when he dumps and ignores you, it'll be worse."

She drew back as if scalded by hot water. "Ugh!"

I felt sorry for Sofia. I wanted her to have what she wanted, but I also knew there was no way she could handle being misused by Ethan. If she didn't like him, and they were just a fling, maybe—but she wanted him hot and heavy. He would crush her entirely.

"Excuse me."

All eyes turned to the dark-timbred announcement at the front of the class, and my entire body lit up at the sight of Dominic.

His gaze carried over the sea of faces, gray eyes locking on mine for what felt like an eternity. My pussy went mad, thumping like a thirsty whore on Main Street. My nipples hardened, heat slapped my body, and chills raced down my flesh. God, he had an unnatural hold on me, and there didn't seem to be anything I could do about it. Not that I wanted to.

"Professor Broward will be late today. So, for this course I'll be filling in for him. It is my impression that you're covering Astronomy 101. Log into your course or take out your textbooks, whichever you prefer."

His eyes dropped from mine as he tapped the computer in front of him. Meanwhile, my eyes covered the length of his muscular build. The button-down shirt was topped with a charcoal twill-tailored Italian vest, and his tie was tucked neatly inside. I squirmed as I assessed him, wishing and wondering simultaneously if I'd ever experience his deep strokes. But that mouth had driven me insane first, then straight to dreamland secondly. Would I even make it through a nightcap with him? I teased my bottom lip with my teeth, imagining his mouth on mine when Emma leaned in and whispered:

"Now that's a professor I would fuck."

Alice chuckled while Sofia nodded.

"Hard, raw, and disgustingly," Emma added.

My pussy was still whacking between my thighs, my clit jumping as if it was waiting to meet up with its master.

Slowly, I turned to eye Emma. "Tell me how you really feel."

She smirked. "I just did." She shrugged. "You asked us

last week if we would fuck an administrator, well..." she let that sentence linger, but Emma had already expressed what I knew.

"He's got to be the hottest man alive," Alice added. Surprised, I glanced at Alice. "What?"

"You rarely speak on men."

"Boys," she reiterated. "I rarely speak on boys because, most of the time, they are not worth mentioning."

I laughed and reached out to high-five her. Our antics brought the attention of Professor Lucas.

"Ladies, is there something you'd like to share with the class?" His deep voice stimulated me, and I squirmed again.

"There is something, but I don't want to share it with either of them," Emma courageously said.

Laughter from the women in the class filled the room, nods and agreements adding to our shared amusement. The boys shook their heads, most of them jealous the professor was getting this attention from us all.

Professor Lucas nodded. "I see. How about you help us with the course, Ms. Taylor, and answer the question that I asked?"

"What was the question?"

More laughter shot up around the room, and I suppressed my smile, though I couldn't hide my blush.

"You seem to find this funny, Ms. Cattaneo. Do you have an answer for me?"

I sucked in my mirth and thought quickly about the question we'd all missed.

"I'll be honest, Professor Lucas, I, too, missed the question. I was much more focused on..."

His gaze darkened, and my nipples hardened. "On what, Ms. Cattaneo?"

I swiped my tongue across my teeth, my skin hot, and nerves jumping across my flesh.

"If you repeat the question, I can answer you."

His gaze dropped to my mouth, lingered, then he rubbed his lips together.

"What is the edge of space termed, and where does it begin?"

I held his gaze as I answered, "The edge of space is referred to as the Kármán line, named after Hungarian-American physicist Theodore von Kármán. It begins sixty-two miles above Earth's atmosphere."

He stared at me for a long minute, then tilted his head. "Well done."

"Do I get a treat for answering correctly?"

His brow rose, but he didn't miss a beat. "See me after class, and I may have something for you."

The women in the class whistled and laughed.

"All right, you've had your fun," he said. "Let's refocus."

He moved on to the next question, raising more issues to which other women who wanted that same attention he'd given me quickly raised their hands.

Emma leaned over. "I think he's proud of you, girl. You better seduce him while you've got the chance."

I smirked and shook my head.

"Seriously, if either of these other bimbos gets to him, it'll be too late. You know men can only focus until their dick is wet."

"If that's true, then I don't want him."

"But he wants you."

My eyes widened, and I turned to stare at her. "Why do you think that?"

"He took his attention off me and gave it to you without you saying a word. And kept it there longer than anyone else. Then invited you to meet with him after class. I'd say he might want a taste. Go test him and see."

I chuckled. "Emma..."

"What?" She sighed. "If you don't do it, let me know, and I will. One of us has to take one for the team, and it might as well be me if not you."

I giggled. "Calm down, please."

The mischievous glint in her eyes told me that she thought her words of encouragement had sealed the deal between me going after Dominic, but she didn't know that I was far, far, ahead of her.

10

Penelope

The clock struck two p.m., and I had never moved so fast to get out of my last class. The halls filled with students, rushing to get to another session or leave campus for the day. I, on the other hand, had other ideas as I cut the corner and entered the open door to Professor Lucas's office.

Click.

His gaze lifted from the computer screen to mine when I shut and locked the door, and without a word, he leaned back in his ergonomic chair, hands sliding behind his head, his gaze crawling over me as I approached.

"Good evening, Professor Lucas." I set my purse and the large black vintage tote bag in which I carried my books on the side of his desk, then perched my ass on the edge.

"Good evening, Ms. Cattaneo."

His deep voice always aroused me, and I preferred it that way.

"You can drop the formal address. It's just me an—"

The toilet flushed in his bathroom, and I stood from his desk and stepped to the side of it as the water in the sink ran.

Seconds later, the door opened, and a woman—Ms. Monroe, one of the student counselors—exited. Her eyes widened when she saw me, then a soft smile replaced her surprise as she strutted over to Dominic.

"I see we have company," her light voice rang. "Or you," she corrected, releasing a flirtatious laugh. Her hand landed on his shoulder, and I couldn't help but size her up.

Ms. Monroe wore a beige ruffled long-sleeve blouse with a mauve pinstripe knee-length skirt. On her feet, three-inch beige heels and jewelry accessorized her wrists, ears, and neck.

Straight auburn hair waved across her shoulders, and the scent she wore was heavily sweet. Ms. Monroe was a beauty, and as long as she stood leaning flirtatiously close to Dominic, the more I considered I was out of my league if she were my competition.

"I...didn't know you were busy," I said, grabbing my tote and purse and quickly turning to leave.

"Well, technically, I'm on my way out the door," Ms. Monroe said. "Are you changing your classes, Ms. Cattaneo?"

"Call me Penelope, please," I said at the door, ready to make my exit.

"Very well," her hand swept down Dominic's arm. "I'll talk to you soon, yes?"

"Yes, ma'am," his said, his voice rich, low, and vibrantly seductive.

A smile lit up her face, and she strutted toward me, making sure to put an extra twist in her steps.

"Penelope," she said, standing before me, "Don't let me stop you from getting advice from Dominic—uh, Professor Lucas," she corrected. "I can talk to him anytime." She patted me on my shoulder like I was a Pomeranian waiting for a treat by the door.

Technically, I had come for a treat, just not one from her.

I smiled, but there was no amusement behind my face. "Have a good day!"

"You too."

After she disappeared, the gusto I'd had disappeared with her. I turned back to look at Dominic, and he remained staring at me with those amazingly gorgeous gray eyes and succulent lips. But I couldn't stand to think I had a chance with him after seeing Ms. Monroe, and much like a fragile pup, I began my retreat, exiting the door.

"Penelope."

I paused, my back to him as I stood, one step into the hallway. "Yes?"

"Come here."

Heat spilled down my body, and I turned back and entered the room but remained by the exit.

"Close the door."

I did what I was told and instinctively turned the lock.

Dominic rose from his seat, and I found myself walking toward him slowly. We met in the middle, and more heat drenched my skin as his gaze ran over my face, mouth, breasts, down my miniskirt and tights.

He reached for my hand and flicked the bags I carried from my grip, causing them to hit the floor. "Is that all it takes?"

My brows arched. "I don't know what you mean."

He squinted. "I don't like a liar, Penelope."

I huffed, closed my eyes, and dropped my head backward, exposing my neck. His arm circled my waist, and he drew me closer, causing an ignition in my core to spark and charge me through and through.

I built that bravado again and responded truthfully, locking eyes with him.

"I stop by to see you because..." I paused. "Well, because I wanted to."

"Not because I told you to?"

I smirked. "You telling me to was the icing on the cake, and it's surprising."

"Why?"

"Since I've tried to get to know you, you've pushed me

away. I hadn't expected you to give into my flirtatiousness."

"So you were flirting with me?"

My smile brightened. "I think you know that."

A low hum, almost like a growl, emerged from his mouth, and the vibration was felt where his touch pressed against my back. "If you stopped by because you wanted to, then why were you leaving?"

I inhaled a deep breath. "If you're fucking Ms. Monroe, there's no reason for me to be here."

He stared at me without a word and I responded again.

"She's, well, beautiful, and closer in age to you. I'm sure she's got it all together and knows what she wants. Pretty irresistible, I think."

"To who? You? Or me?"

"I..." I pressed my lips together and squinted at him. "Is that a trick question?"

"A question is a question, never a trick." Without allowing me to reply, he continued. "Beauty is in the eye of the beholder, Penelope. You're gorgeous—a goddess, to me, intelligent—which I knew but witnessing in real time today aroused me. I've been inside your home, seen your neighborhood. It looks like you've got it all together. So, what would make Ms. Monroe better?"

He had me there. I was stumped. A smirk slid across his face but just as quickly, he dropped it.

"The truth is, I am seven years your senior, possess

more experience in a lot of ways than you. Women from all walks of life are attracted to me. Will you run every time you see one flirting or will you stay?"

"I wasn't running, just merely giving you your space."

"Liar."

I sucked in a breath. "I wasn't."

We had a standoff and I internally coached myself not to fold. A smirk creased his face, then:

"Did you sleep well last night?"

"Very well." I rubbed my lips together. "Could've been earthshattering if you would've stayed."

"And if I would have, how would my presence have been earthshattering?"

I opened my mouth, but words evaded me, more so because they were hot and nasty, much like Emma had said before.

"Don't hold back."

I swallowed and leaned closer, my hands touching his torso and holding there. His gaze dropped, with eyes watching me through heavy lids.

"I wanted you to fuck me, Dominic."

"Wanted?"

I panted, my chest rising and falling as if breathless because he made me spell it out. "Want. I want you to fuck me."

"How can you be sure you're prepared for me, Penelope?"

My body trembled, heat slipped down the seat of my panties, and my panting accelerated.

"I'm not a timid, breakable toy, Dominic, regardless of how you think I can't handle you. I can."

His lids turned into slits, but his eyes weren't closed completely. Dominic's hand moved from my back. With his left, he gripped my waist. With his right, he slid his big hand underneath my skirt, inside my tights, covered my pussy with his palm, slipped a finger inside me, then lifted me with a grip of my pussy.

"Aaaaaah," I gasped, eyes wide and heart ricocheting like an impassioned pistol.

My hands dropped to his shoulders when he elevated me, and we moved to his desk where he perched my ass on the top. That thick finger moved in and out of me. Shivers sliced up and down my body, as I was drenched in heat. My nipples tightened hard, and he lifted my shirt with his other hand, pulled my bra down, and blew over my nubs. The piercing, pleasurable pain sensation scattered around the hard nipple, and the sensory made me moan.

"Mmmmmm." I bit my lip, bucked my hips against his finger-fucking, and arched as the sensations lit up my body. "Ooooh, sssssss, Dominic!"

He leaned over me and whispered in my ear. "Shuuu-uuuuush. Take it without sound."

I panted. "Hooow..."

"Use your inside voice."

I squealed with my mouth closed, and he bit into my

neck and slipped another finger inside me. My mouth opened to squeal, and he lifted my head and covered my lips, giving me his tongue to suck to muffle my screams.

His cinnamon taste filled me, and I sucked while he finger-fucked, and when I thought it couldn't get any more fulfilling, his thumb grazed across my clit. Dominic moved his fingers like a master pianist who used each digit to drive a different sensation with the intent to cause the same exploding outcome.

Me? I was bucking, shuddering, moaning, sucking his tongue, and gripping his shoulders like a woman locked inside a sensual virtual reality.

What had come over me?

What had he done to me?

My toes curled, my orgasm on edge; I came on his fingers, my body jerking on his desk as I shouted down his throat. Dominic sucked my mouth, bit my lip, then left a hot trail of kisses down my neck as I took in my first breath of unused oxygen.

"Oh my God." I blinked, my vision off but refocusing second by second. Dominic pulled his hand from my pussy and slid the fingers into his mouth.

His eyes closed, broad shoulders rising on an inhale, and an animalistic snarl moved through him.

"Hmmmmm."

When his eyes opened, he gazed at me for so long that I felt bewitched where I was. "Take a trip with me."

"Okay," I purred.

He smirked. "I haven't told you where we're going."

"I don't really care."

"What I said still stands. The longer you're around me, the more danger you're in. Do you still want to go?"

"Yes."

"Are you not afraid, Penelope?"

"You'll protect me."

He locked his jaw and stared. "Do you know what that looks like?"

"Your protection?"

"Yes."

"No... but, still, I don't care."

His nostrils flared and I wanted him so bad that my pulse quickened. His fingers tapped down my face, then he moved away from me, opened one of his drawers, and pulled out a set of keys.

When he drew me to an upright sitting position, I noticed the keys were mine. My eyes widened.

"Your car is parked in your paid parking spot. Your belongings are on the seat. Nothing has been stolen from your bank account."

I gasped. "How did you do this?"

"It's better if you don't ask me questions like that."

We stared at one another, and I nodded. "When do we leave?"

"This weekend. We'll be gone for seven days. Plan accordingly."

I nodded and closed the gap between us, my lips

landing on his mouth. He inhaled deeply as our kiss took on a life of its own, our tongues clashing and mouths crushing.

My core ignited when he pulled away. "Go."

I lingered, but his next command felt like a warning. "Now."

I saw a change in him, something perilously close to alarm. My legs moved, I grabbed my belongings and left his office—but long after I was gone, Dominic was still with me.

11

Dominic

The helicopter's blades sliced through the crisp winter air. Beside me, Penelope's presence was a soothing solace, her eyes wide with awe as we approached the secluded island owned by the Lucas Cosa Nostra, my favorite sanctuary.

The open waters we crossed were a canvas of deep blues and greens, the waves cresting and falling like the breathing of a slumbering giant. The sun was a muted orb in the winter sky, casting a silvery light over the seascape, turning the water into a shimmering expanse that stretched endlessly toward the horizon.

As we drew nearer, the island revealed itself—a lush oasis amidst the vastness of the sea. It was a jewel of nature, an untamed beauty I had tamed just enough to call my own. Forests of pine and olive trees clung to the rugged cliffs, their branches dusted with a light frost that sparkled under the sun's touch. The air was scented with the sea's briny tang and the woods' earthy fragrance.

I leaned closer to Penelope, my voice a low rumble over the hum of the helicopter. "The only way in or out is by helicopter."

Her eyes widened. "What about by boat?"

"There is no way to dock by boat outside of the island, but there is a yacht for the purposes of entertainment."

Her brows rose. "I supposed making the helicopter the only entrance was done on purpose?"

"Yes."

"Why?"

"So it will be revealed ahead of time when danger lurks."

A shudder slid over her shoulders. "As in when someone shows up uninvited?"

"Exactly that."

You've mentioned danger before. What kind of danger?"

"Does it matter?"

She shrugged. "Danger is danger, I guess."

I smirked. "Yes," I drawled. "It is."

"And what happens if someone tries to breach your island without prior approval?"

"I make the sea their new home."

Her eyes widened, and she stared at me. I saw apprehension in her soft, mystic eyes. Penelope was wondering what she'd gotten herself into. But it was far too late to think twice. I'd tasted her, and now, she was mine.

THE ESTATE WAS AN ARCHITECTURAL MARVEL, a fusion of modern luxury and classic Italian elegance. The main house, sprawling and grand, was built of warm stone and rich, dark wood, its large windows reflecting the winter sky. Red-hued terra cotta roofs adorned each building against the verdant landscape.

The helicopter descended, the blades sending a flurry of snow swirling around us as we landed on a helipad nestled in the gardens. I glanced at Penelope, her face alight with wonder, and felt a surge of satisfaction.

This was my world, and I was sharing it with her. While I controlled what she saw, I knew having her around was playing a dangerous game.

WE STEPPED out onto the helipad, the crunch of snow underfoot breaking the silence of the secluded haven. The gardens, even in winter, revealed meticulous care. Bare, twisting vines of what would be vibrant rose bushes in spring lined the pathways, their thorns glistening with tiny droplets of melted frost. Statues of marble, remnants of a long-forgotten era, stood straight amidst the sleeping flora, their expressions serene under the weight of time.

A short walk brought us to the vineyards, rows upon rows of grapevines standing dormant, their branches bare and waiting for the warmth of spring to awaken them. I watched Penelope as she trailed her fingers over the rough bark, a look of quiet contemplation on her face.

Beyond the vineyards lay the main house. As we approached, the details of its splendor became apparent. Intricate carvings adorned the doorways and windows, scenes of Italian folklore and history etched into the stone. The large doors opened to a grand foyer, its high ceilings, and open space a welcoming embrace.

I led Penelope through the house, each room a blend of opulence and comfort. The furniture was plush and inviting, the walls adorned with art that spoke of my refined taste. Fireplaces crackled in every room, their warmth making you forget about the winter chill outside.

The tour ended at the back of the house, where large windows offered a panoramic view of the island. The sea stretched out before us, a vast, undulating entity of its own being.

I stood beside Penelope, my gaze lingering on her profile, the way her eyes reflected the beauty of the world I had brought her into on the surface.

At that moment, I felt a sense of peace, a rare respite from the duties and demands of my life as the underboss of the Lucas Cosa Nostra and the Black Rose. I inhaled that peace and had wrestled with it in the beginning because it was foreign and unrealistic.

But the more Penelope refused to leave me, the more I reveled in its splendor in the relaxing essence of its powerful magic. Against my better judgment, I'd allowed it, and now, in this moment, I lived a dream I'd wanted to make a reality all those years ago when I was just a boy. To be normal and captivated by a woman who shared my captivation; tucked away at the serene beauty of a hidden paradise.

Unfortunately, that wasn't my reality, but I would pretend as long as this trip would last.

"This is an amazing fortress," she said. "It feels like something out of a fairy tale."

I smirked. "Beauty and the Beast, perhaps."

Her lips spread into a smile, and laughter shuffled from her—that sound that tingled the soles of my feet and accelerated my heartbeat.

Long lashes fluttered over at me. "Perhaps, but then, if you recall that fairy tale, the Beast rained hell upon anyone around him because of the life he'd been forced to live, not of his own doing."

I inhaled a deep breath, my jaw locking. *Penelope saw me.*

I couldn't ignore that. She didn't know how much of a beast I was, yet still, she saw me without witnessing my hell and had already decided I was worthy of...something better than the darkness that consumed me.

"Yes, but that didn't take away the pain he'd caused. Or, the hell he'd rained, as you put it."

"And still, he was redeemed."

Silence moved between us as our gazes locked.

I smiled. "Are you hungry?"

"A little."

"We've got a party to attend, so I hope you feel like dancing."

Her face brightened. "Dancing? You? Oh, I've got to see this."

I laughed. "Why is that so surprising?"

"I could only picture you standing in a quiet corner, brooding." She imitated my face and I howled, my amusement heightened.

"Is that how I look?"

"Yeah. And it's all sexy and shit."

I reached out and pinched her face. "Is that why you won't leave my side because I'm all sexy and shit?"

"No." Her smile faded, and sentiments of kindness filled her eyes. "My soul connects with yours. I feel... drawn to you, if that makes sense."

"It doesn't make a bit of sense considering who you are and who I am."

"But you don't know who I am, Dominic."

If we were talking about details, she had me there. We had yet to broach that conversation because

I'd been too busy trying to will her away from me. But if we were talking about souls, I assumed hers would clash violently with the chaos that resided in mine.

Fortunately, that had yet to happen. Penelope's light was the peace that made me act out of my norms; it calmed me and I'd yet to figure out if that was a good thing or not.

"You're right."

She wiggled her brows. "I am."

"Not entirely; so half-correct.

She giggled heavily.

"What I don't know is—who are the Bonnie and Clyde you referred to as your parents?"

She sucked in her laughter and rolled her eyes. "Gosh." She took her eyes beyond the window to the horizon. "They were my favorite people when I was a preteen, but their love for gunplay, robbing banks, and murdering anyone who dared stand in their way took precedence over raising me."

"If they didn't raise you, then who?"

Her entire body language changed. The emotion emptied out of her eyes, leaving them vacant and cold. She folded her arms, turned from the window, and strolled away.

Her change in demeanor kept me intrigued, and I followed her but didn't rush her response.

"Benjamin. *Non è degno dell'aria che respira.*"

I paused at her fluently spoken Italian. *He is unworthy of the air he breathes*, she'd said.

"Non sapevo che parlassi la lingua."

She faced me. "I don't. I mean, I do speak the language, but I'm a bit rusty as I don't put it to good use most of the time."

"Most of the time?"

"It comes out when I'm angry."

"So, you're angry now?"

She sucked in a deep breath. "I don't care to talk about Benjamin."

"Then let's change the subject."

"I want you to know who he is first, so I never have to bring him up again."

I stared at her quietly, assessing the tremble in her fingers and the unease of her voice.

"Go on."

"He's my uncle, who raised me and molested me every time there was a thunderstorm."

My gut tightened, and rage filled me to capacity.

"He made sure to wait until the storm so my cries would be muffled, and the neighbors wouldn't hear."

Her eyes clouded with tears.

"He—"

"Stop. Please."

"You need to know."

"The only thing I need to know is if his last name is Cattaneo."

"Why?"

"It's better if you don't ask me questions like that, Penelope."

She closed her lips tight and calmed her breathing.

"They love him. You can't get him in trouble."

"And by they, you mean your parents?"

"Yes. Well, Salvatore—Benjamin's brother."

"Does your father know about his brother's sins?"

"No."

She'd just unknowingly saved her parent's life.

"If he did, he wouldn't love him anymore."

She let out a ragged breath. "If no other lives have to be ruined besides mine, I'm willing to live with that. Besides, my parents are in prison. They would be in agony to hear it, knowing they could do nothing about it." She hesitated. "You know what, never mind what I said. My life isn't ruined. I shouldn't have said that. I've overcome it and thankfully have wonderful friends, another wonderful uncle, wealth, and a good life."

"Except when it storms."

She closed her mouth tight and didn't utter another word.

"Is his last name Cattaneo?"

"I'll tell you if you promise not to get him in trouble."

"I can't promise that."

"Then I can't tell you."

The standoff between us went on for longer than I liked. I let the silence linger until she finally spoke.

"Caruso."

I squinted. "Caruso is Italian. You have Italian blood in your lineage?"

"Yes."

Penelope was becoming more and more interesting. But Cattaneo nor Caruso sounded familiar to the Italians I knew, and I knew them all—mostly.

"Hmmm."

"Can we change the subject now?"

"Yes." She nodded, relief washing over her face.

"Let me introduce you to someone." I led Penelope into the grand palace kitchen. As we entered, the staff greeted us formally.

"Mr. Lucas, it's wonderful to have you back in Italy."

"Speak English, Edgar."

"Very well. Greetings, it's wonderful to have you back in Italy." He glanced at Penelope. "Who do we have the pleasure of serving this afternoon?"

"Ms. Cattaneo—"

She broke in. "Please, call me Penelope."

I paused, then regarded Edgar. "You heard the lady."

"Penelope, it is nice to meet your acquaintance."

"It's nice to meet you too, Edgar."

"My staff and I were informed of your visit, and we have prepared a few lunch options for your choosing."

"I'm sure it's delicious, whatever it is," Penelope murmured with a smile.

116

"You're very kind. Would you like a tour of the kitchen?"

She glanced at me. "Do we have time?"

"Yes."

Her bright eyes moved back to Edgar. "Yes, I would."

Edgar nodded. "Follow me."

I watched them walk away and enter the double doors of the kitchen.

Inhaling a deep breath, I turned and exited, walking the long stretch of my palace corridor where I entered my office.

The tall mahogany door swung closed behind me, and I strolled over Saxony carpets moved behind my desk, and powered on the computer. It took a ten-minute search on the dark web to find Benjamin Caruso.

In Philadelphia.

I tapped the keys, and the government satellite I hacked zoomed in on Benjamin, sleeping soundly in his bedroom. He was obviously not a man concerned with his well-being as there was no security in place. The front and back doors could be picked easily, as they were equipped with the cheap generic locks that supposedly kept intruders out.

No...

Benjamin slept like a man without worries or fear. But when his eyes rested on my face, he would fear me.

I surveyed his street—the intersections, crosswalks, local traffic, and police presence.

Five minutes later, I had everything I needed. I checked my search history, ensuring it self-destructed within sixty seconds, exactly as I had programmed it to do whenever I accessed the server.

A minute later, there was no trail left behind. I sat in silence with my thoughts, noting that going after Benjamin was not a part of my original plans, and considered the ways it could backfire.

I came up empty. But there were always possibilities. For this excursion, however, I would deal with unpredictable challenges should they arise.

Switching gears, I checked the palace hosting the masquerade ball we were attending tonight to get a glimpse of how tight the security would be. Attending as the underboss of the Lucas Cosa Nostra with Penelope presented a risk. Luckily for me, everyone in our underworld knew not to discuss business matters in front of women.

Still, I knew someone would want to pull me to the side to ask about something, even though this was primarily a social gathering for other members of the underworld to hold small talk while tightening our alliances.

For me, however, I needed to get my eyes on the operations of the Cappalli crime family. Vito Cappalli was the boss, and his unwavering dominance at the port had kept Dameon's business thriving for the last half a century. It was time for his entire family to meet the Black Rose.

The Niccolò family would soon follow.

KNOCK. *Knock.*

I hit the escape key, and my screen blackened. Standing, I strolled to the door and opened it.

"Sorry to bother you, sir."

"Alexus, you know I am not to be disturbed when I'm in my study."

"Yes, I apologize, but the lady you brought...Penelope...she refuses to eat without you."

I stared at him, inhaled deeply, and nodded. "I'll be there momentarily."

"Yes, sir."

I watched him walk away, turned to look at the computer, and left the office. In the dining hall, I approached the royal table where she sat and stood on the opposite side.

"I thought you were hungry?"

"I am." Her gaze was steady.

"Then why aren't you eating?"

She huffed. "I don't want to eat alone, Dominic. I came here with you. I want to eat with you."

I lifted my chin and stared her down. "Is that it?"

"For the moment."

I glanced at the food she hadn't touched. "How long have you been sitting here without eating?"

She shrugged. "Maybe fifteen minutes."

"I see."

I looked toward Chef Edgar, who stood at the entrance. "Edgar—"

"Can we..." Penelope broke in. I glanced back at her as she continued to speak. "I'm sorry. I didn't mean to interrupt, but can we sit at a more intimate table?" She pushed her palms together. "Shorter, so we can be closer. There's no need for this grand table."

"Would you like anything else?"

Tilting her head, she thought for a moment, her lips curving into a crescent smile. "No."

"Edgar, please set lunch for two at the console table."

"Yes, sir."

I strolled to Penelope's side and held my hand out. Her fingers linked with mine, and a spark of heat dropped straight to my dick. I closed my eyes, absorbed that warmth, and guided her to our table.

12

Penelope

"Oxtail osso buco on a bed of Mashed Potatoes," Edgar announced.

"This looks and smells delicious."

"I hope you enjoy it, Penelope." Edgar glanced at Dominic. "Sir." He tilted his head and disappeared inside the kitchen.

Wine glasses were filled halfway by other servers and announced in the same manner as the meal.

I smirked over at Dominic. He was different—a bit more open than before, and I wondered if it was because he liked me now or if he simply needed a date to this party he mentioned.

"Do you pray?" I asked.

"To whom?"

Silence settled over us, and I blinked, not expecting his response.

"To...God?"

"Would you like to pray over our food, Penelope?"

"Yes. If that is okay with you."

He nodded once, and I reached for his hands. He regarded my fingers and didn't reach his hand out to meet mine. I pulled my bottom lip in with my teeth and nodded. Prayer seemed to be out of his norm. But that could be changed. I dropped my eyes and left my hands open as I blessed our food.

When I finished, I opened my eyes to find his fingers mere inches from touching mine. A smile filled my face, and I grabbed his hands.

"It's okay to touch me. You should know that by now."

"I know," he drawled.

"If you know, why did you stop so close to my fingers?"

"Because I wanted to."

We watched each other for a minute, and I accepted his response. I took the first bite of oxtail, and the flavor melted in my mouth.

"Oh...this is divine."

"I'm glad you like it."

"Mm-hmm."

We ate in silence for a few minutes, but the thoughts I'd entertained while given a tour of the kitchen wouldn't let my mind rest.

"Tell me about your family, Dominic."

He dabbed his mouth with a napkin. "No."

I choked on mashed potatoes and patted my chest.

Lifting a glass of water, I swallowed the lump lodged in my throat. "No?"

He stared at me, refusing to repeat himself.

"Why not?"

"Because I said so."

"How are we supposed to get to know each other?"

"My family doesn't represent me, Penelope." He uttered those words with such finality that I had to believe him.

"But, you don't have any siblings you're close to that you love?"

"Do you?"

"No. Unfortunately, I'm an only child."

"Mmmmm."

"Now it's your turn."

He gazed at me for so long that I thought he'd burn a hole into me. "Sisters. Four." He lifted his fork to eat.

"What are their names?"

"Why?"

I gawked. "Dominic."

He smirked. "Is that your stern voice?"

I suppressed a smile. "It can get worse if you don't play fair."

"The games I want to play with you do not consist of talk of my *famiglia*."

A string of palpable heat coursed down my flesh. I licked my lips.

"Yes, well, ditto."

He held me in that dark gaze and almost effectively changed the subject, but I pulled myself from his lure.

"Sisters. Names," I said.

He ate food, sipped his wine, and ate some more. "Luna, Gabriella, Alessandra, Franca."

"Those are beautiful names."

He nodded.

"Is Luna the oldest?"

"Of my *sorella*, yes."

"Are you close?"

"Yes."

I smiled, imagining Dominic with a close sister.

"Did you all get in trouble when you were younger, or was she one of those siblings who followed you around?"

"She's what I imagine a younger brother would be. Bold, a leader, unforgiving, protective."

"Unforgiving? She sounds as intense as you."

"Almost."

I smirked. "I'd love to meet her one day."

"Why?"

"Maybe we'd have something in common; who knows?"

A deep laugh belted from his gut, and I frowned. "What's so funny?"

"I can assure you, Penelope, there's no commonality between you and Luna."

"How can you say that when—"

"Trust me. I know."

"Hmmmmm." I folded my arms. "You know, I can be a badass, too."

More laughter floated from him, and I knew then he still saw me as this perfect little princess.

I pursed my lips and stared at him, my gaze stern.

Noticing my annoyance, Dominic dabbed his mouth again, rose from his seat, and walked around the table to my side. He pulled out a chair beside me and sat, bringing the aromatic scent of his allure right under my nose.

"You don't need to be a badass, Penelope. You need to be *you*. That is why you're here with me and why I can't manage to stay away, even though I should."

Tingles sporadically surged over my skin. "Are you saying you like me?"

He held my attention. "I do."

A silly-ass smile spread across my lips. I couldn't hold it back if I tried. Simultaneously, my stomach flipped, and a rush of emotions hit me at once.

"I like you too, Dominic. A lot."

"Hmmmmm," he growled. "You've made better choices in your life, I'm sure."

My eyes widened. "Don't say that. Why do you think so poorly of yourself?"

"You've misunderstood me. I'm a catch, girl."

I laughed heartily.

"In another life," he added.

And that sucked the wind right out of me.

"If it's that bad, you can always change your life. Our

decisions, paths, and futures are not final until we die." I leaned in and placed a kiss on his lips. "Don't count yourself out just yet. I think being with you will be one of the best decisions I've made if you stop pushing me away."

"You should be a politician."

I frowned. "Why?"

"You give me hope when there is none."

My mouth dropped. "Well, thanks, I think."

"We're attending a masquerade ball in four hours."

I gasped and squealed all at once. "On the arm of the finest dark prince in all the land," I purred.

He bit his bottom lip, trying to suppress his smile. "Yes, well, that is not too far from the truth."

"I bet it isn't, because who is better than you?"

"Is that a question I'm supposed to answer?"

"No."

"Good."

I loved his conversation...when he gave it to me.

"You'll need to change your appearance and use an alias. Will you be okay with that?"

Surprised, I nodded. "Whatever you need."

"Mmmmmm."

"Who am I?"

"Caterina Bianchi."

"That's a beautiful name. Does it come from someone you know?"

He was in his head for a while before he spoke.

"No. When I was a boy, I'd entertain silly thoughts of

a family. Caterina would be my daughter's name if that life had been for me."

"Wow. I will hold the name close to my heart."

He nodded once. "You'll have a small team of helpers to get you ready. Everything you need for your transformation is available to you."

"Is there anything else I should know?"

"The ball we're attending is hosted by a powerful family. They are not as relaxed as you."

"Oh. So, should I be uptight or be myself?"

He smirked. "I'll leave that up to you. I feel like you can improvise."

I nodded. "Sure."

"You should finish eating. It's going to be a long night."

He left my side of the table and reclaimed his seat. We finished our food, and now my mind was filled with thoughts of what the masquerade ball would entail.

13

Dominic

T he floor-to-ceiling windows gave me a panoramic view of the sunset. We were one hour away from Riccardo Niccolò's masquerade ball, and I had everything I needed to make my attendance worthwhile.

"That's a beautiful sunset."

I turned to Penelope's voice and experienced a surge in my heart's tempo at the divine way she took on her transformation.

She stood confident with her chin lifted; red lipstick heightened her beauty against the fringed, sequined black body-complementing dress. A wavy burnt orange wig fell over her shoulders down to her perky nipples, and red high-heeled open-toe shoes adorned her feet. On her face a black sequin feathered masked covered her eyes and nose.

I strolled to her, carefully assessing Penelope. "Still a goddess."

She smiled. "You like this?"

"You complement the look excellently."

"Which means you like it."

I chuckled. "Yes, I like it, Penelope."

She blushed. "Just wanted to hear you say it."

"I gathered." I slipped a finger down her face, and her blush deepened. Even now, when I was on the brink of an important mission, I wanted to shove my dick inside her. To resist, I kept my control intact, but it had been slowly eroding every time she was near.

"Bianca," I beckoned.

Bianca entered the room quickly. "Yes, sir?"

"Cover her tattoo and bring her coat."

"Yes, sir."

Looking back at Penelope, I assessed her again. "Are you ready, Penelope?"

"Who?"

I smiled. "Good girl."

THE ROAD WAS GRIDLOCKED with black luxury vehicles, and when we finally made it to the front, Penelope slipped her hand in mine.

"You will do fine. I'm certain of it."

A small smile crossed her lips, and I kissed her forehead then added the phantom mask I'd decided to wear for the night on my face. The door opened, and I exited, turned, held my hand out, and helped her out to stand at my side. In the distance, flashes from awaiting photographers burst as they captured images of attendees.

I understood this came with the gathering of a party such as this. Still, I hated it even if they didn't know who I was because of my mask. Moving with long strides, I led Penelope past the photographers, who were busy capturing others, entering the palace without pause.

Next to me, Penelope's strides matched mine, and I was pleased that she understood my plight.

We approached a guard as tall as my six feet seven inches. He tapped the screen on an electronic display podium.

"Enter your key."

I entered the Lucas Cosa Nostra code, and the screen lit up green, then shifted to another command.

"Retina scan."

I leaned forward and held still as the device completed its scan. My name slipped across the screen.

"Welcome, Mr. Lucas."

I nodded as he stepped out of our way, and we entered.

"That was intense," Penelope murmured.

"It is a normal part of the life we live."

"I didn't think you were too involved with your father's lifestyle."

I paused and looked at her. "Do you know who Dameon is? Really?"

"I mean, he's a billionaire, kinda scary. There are rumors he's a mafia don."

I smirked, and we continued to move. "And do you believe the rumors?"

"Honestly, I don't know what to think. He's clearly a billionaire, but a mafia don seems like a stretch."

"Why?"

"It's a plot right out of the movies. I know dons are real or have been real in the past, but you don't hear much about them in real life today."

A server approached us with a tray of champagne.

"Would you like something to drink?" I asked her.

"Yes."

I took two flutes from the tray and handed her one. She took a sip.

"Hmmm, that's tasty."

"I take it you like it?"

"Not as much as your wine, but yes."

I nodded. "Noted."

"So, is your father a mafia don?"

"Yes." Her eyes widened, and I continued. "He has security, lives on a compound, kills men when he needs to get rid of them, lures beautiful women inside and fucks them as he wishes, and he's run his empire for over fifty years selling a profusion of drugs to addicts on the streets."

She stared at me for a long, silent few minutes, and

then laughter burst from her mouth. I watched her squirm in ticklish fever as amusement struck her repeatedly.

"Oh gosh, that was so far-fetched! You don't expect me to believe that, do you?"

"I'm his protégé. I would know."

"I thought we weren't lying to each other?"

"You asked, and I answered."

"Is this a part of your make-believe cover tonight?"

"You're the only one undercover tonight, goddess."

She stared at me in disbelief, and I smirked, glancing away in time to see an approaching figure.

"I must say, Dominic, I didn't expect to see you here tonight." Riccardo Niccolò held out a hand, and I accepted it with a brisk handshake.

"I apologize for the lack of RSVP. The opportunity presented itself at the last minute." I glanced at Penelope. "Riccardo, this is my date, Caterina Bianchi—Caterina, Riccardo Niccolò, the most important man in the room tonight."

"Outside of you, you mean," she purred.

I stared at her mouth, smirked, and looked back at Riccardo, who seemed to be captivated by Penelope, if the way his gaze fixed on her inquisitively was any indication.

His polite laugh was a farce that I accepted dealing with for the moment.

"Caterina..." he drawled. "That's a beautiful name."

"Thank you, Riccardo—or should I call you Niccolò?"

Her pronunciation surprised me, as most got it wrong on their first try.

"Riccardo is fine. Thank you for joining us tonight."

"It was my pleasure when Dominic asked."

"Mmmm, and how did you two meet?"

"That's a funny story. I promised a friend I would join her bachelorette auction for charity, and Dominic just happened to place the winning bid."

"You're right. That is funny but not as unexpected as you might think."

Her smile dropped a bit. "Why do you say that?"

"Women flocked to Dominic like a magnet, but he prefers the chase. To pay for a lady means you belong to him on his time. What could he have done to keep you, I wonder?"

"Who says he kept me? Maybe it was me that kept him."

Riccardo laughed and pointed at Penelope while talking to me. "I like her."

I kept my face neutral and remembered why I was here. Riccardo was an ally, but he had a habit of trying to embarrass me since I was a boy. I would punch him in his throat and cut off his oxygen if matters weren't more pressing. There would be time for that in the near future.

My eyes landed on Vito Cappalli at a table on the left side of the room. Nearing a draped corridor – the underboss Antonio Cappalli exited.

"Can you point me in the direction of the restroom?" I

asked.

"If I can get a dance with Caterina."

I gazed at Penelope, and she nodded. "Of course."

"Perfect," Riccardo said, gazing at her like a hungry lion. "Straight to the left, the dim hallway through the draperies."

"I'll return shortly."

Penelope nodded, and I excused myself.

Slipping away, I navigated the throng of opulence, my steps intentional and my mind focused on one objective. The grandeur around me faded into a blur, and in the shadows of the corridor, I found Antonio Cappalli, his back to me, engrossed in a hushed conversation with a cell phone at his ear.

I edged closer with a small device nestled securely in my palm. It was no larger than a button, a marvel of technology designed for stealth. This moment presented itself like a carefully planned mission, and it was important I executed it now because there were no promises that another chance would arise.

I brushed past Antonio, feigning a momentary loss of balance. My fingers deftly planted the device on the hem of his jacket. It adhered, invisible to the untrained eye.

"*Mi scusi*," I muttered, offering a brief nod before continuing on.

Antonio barely acknowledged me, his attention unyielding from his discussion. I didn't look back, confident in my sleight of hand. The device would capture every word and whisper, transmitting directly to my secure line. It was a necessary intrusion, a way to stay one step ahead in a game where I was the dealer and executioner.

I veered toward the restroom, entered, and approached the sink. I lifted the mask and splashed cold water on my face, staring at my reflection. I couldn't help but feel the isolation of my position. Power, wealth, influence, and dominance were all shackles in their own right.

Exiting the restroom, I composed myself and readjusted my mask, keeping it firmly in place.

I had to return to Penelope, to Riccardo, to the gilded cage of the party. But my mind was already sifting through the information that would pour into my lap because of Antonio's disregard.

———

RICCARDO SPUN Penelope around the dance floor, her laughter light and carefree. For a fleeting moment, I envied her oblivion, the simplicity of a life untouched by the shadows I navigated daily. But this was my reality, a world where trust was a luxury and every alliance was laced with potential betrayal.

"Having fun, I see," I remarked, reclaiming Penelope's hand as the dance ended.

She beamed up at me, her eyes sparkling with unguarded joy. "It's been wonderful, thank you."

Riccardo offered a knowing smile, his gaze sharp. "You two make a striking pair. Dominic, you've always had a taste for the exquisite."

I inclined my head, acknowledging the compliment and the hidden barbs that came with it. "Thank you, Riccardo. Shall we?" I gestured to Penelope, ready to escort her from the dance floor.

As we mingled through the crowd, the tiny device securely attached to Antonio Cappalli's jacket was ever-present in my mind. It reminded me of the dual life I led, the constant balancing act between the man I presented to the world and the one who operated in the shadows.

Penelope's presence at my side had a calming effect on me, whereas when I was alone at these gatherings, every eye watched me to see what the brooding infamous Dominic Lucas was up to. It was one of the reasons I knew she would be perfect as a plus one tonight—that, and keeping an eye on her was becoming my obsession.

She laughed as we engaged in light conversation, but I remained alert, always listening, always watching. In this world, I could never let my guard down, not even for a moment. Being the Black Rose and underboss simultaneously was proof that one never knew who lurked in their vicinity and what their intentions were.

When we got a moment alone, Penelope leaned in. "I was shocked that Riccardo knew who you were immediately. Your presence seems to be a secret to everyone else here. The mask is doing its job, I think."

"Yes. The theme is why I'm in attendance. Otherwise, the majority of the room would rush us, and we'd have a line forming where most would want to have a formal chitchat about everything and nothing at all."

"But Riccardo—"

"Knew who I was because this is his party and he was alerted the minute my retina scan cleared."

"Ah...that makes sense."

"If he had not approached me, I would've thought he was off his game."

She chuckled. "I must say, it's nice to see you in this element, Profes—Dominic."

I *tsked*. "Careful."

"I apologize."

She went mute, and I watched her for the better part of a minute. "Was this a bad idea?"

"No. No," she repeated. "I'm almost used to calling you Dominic alone."

"What can I do to seal it in your mind?"

She gave me a risqué look. "I've got an idea."

My nostrils flared, and I swallowed the remaining champagne in my glass, set the flute aside, lifted Penelope, tossed her over my shoulder, and headed to the exit.

Still, I didn't miss the look in Riccardo's eyes.

What was that...tension?

I would put it away for now, but stored it in a mental file to be assessed later.

14

Penelope

Our mouths crashed together the instant we were inside the backseat of the limo. My ass didn't have a chance to touch the seat before Dominic dragged me underneath him on the wide leather bench.

"Mmmmm," I moaned as his mouth inhaled my tongue, sending riveting blankets of heat over my skin. I gripped the collar of his coat, pulled it apart, and slipped my arms over his shoulders as he ground between my legs.

"Yessssss."

His dick was hard as a brick. I could feel the weight of it through his pants.

"I want it in my mouth."

He nibbled down my neck, over my now-exposed shoulders, but I'd planned to get what I wanted this time.

Dominic had done a perfect job of giving me just enough without giving me everything.

This time, I was going for it all. I pushed his chest, and he rose up off me and sat back. My fingers fumbled with his Ferragamo leather belt. One twist to loosen his pants, and I surpassed the zipper, reached in, and leaned over as I pulled out his dick.

"*Madre di Dio,*" I said.

A thick, veiny shaft swatted at me and popped me in the mouth. I laughed and purred simultaneously while sizing up the length of his erection.

"Have a change of heart, goddess?"

I needed to somehow create more space in the back of my throat, but I wasn't about to stop now.

I fisted his dick but couldn't close my hand around his girth. Still, I made do, driving my hand up and down, sliding from the seat to my knees, where I felt like I had the most leverage.

I sucked the tip, then opened my mouth and sucked as much of him as I could to the back of my open throat.

"Mmmmmmmm." I was instantly wet, my pussy thumping wildly as I became fully aroused.

Dominic reached for my head, removing my wig and pulling out the pins that held my hair up. My hair fell to my shoulders, and he slid his fingers into my curls, gripped my scalp, and guided my direction.

His dick was heavy, and smooth against my tongue with a fresh out-the-shower scent. Each time I came up I took him deeper—deeper, and then his guidance became faster.

"Mmmmmm..." I bobbed and sucked, moved my head in circles, gagged, and swallowed the saliva that covered his erection when I heard him moan.

"Penelope..."

I glanced up to see his head fall back, his pleasure motivating me to go deeper, faster. I choked repeatedly, my eyes watered, and for what felt like thirty seconds, I couldn't breathe because my mouth and throat were clogged with dick.

"Ah!" I sucked off his shaft and inhaled a huge intake of breath, then dove back as deep as I could go and sucked his cock like I was about to win a marathon.

"Grgggggh!"

My nipples hardened, and the pulsation between my thighs ramped up, igniting my desire and keeping me steady.

I stroked him and sucked him, teased the tip, and let him fuck my mouth with upsurging hip strokes.

"Uh!"

I felt his hand tremble on my scalp, and he didn't warn me, but I knew he was coming.

"Mmmmm!"

He coated my palette with light, sweet, flavorful nut. It ran down the side of my mouth and the back of my throat for what felt like forever.

I was shocked at the amount of it all, making me wonder if it had been a while since he'd had an orgasm.

I didn't have much time to consider it. Dominic snatched me off the floorboard, spread me wide on my back, and tore a hole through my pantyhose.

"Is this shiny, wet pussy all for me?"

"Yes."

"And who owns this pussy?"

"You."

"Who?"

"Dominic," I panted.

He sucked in a mouthful of my clit, and my legs were already quivering.

"Ahhhh..." My head fell back, and he didn't give me mercy, sucking and licking, flipping his tongue around my aroused flesh.

I came almost instantly from being heavily stimulated. My heart slammed, and I squirmed to get away from him, my flesh sensitive.

"Where are you going, Penelope?"

I panted. "Give me a second."

"One."

He reached for me again, and I squealed as the limo pulled onto the rooftop where the helicopter waited on the helipad.

A growl moved through him. "You get a fifteen-minute break. Lucky you."

I yelped as he grabbed me and hauled me out of the limo toward our waiting transportation.

I THINK I stopped breathing when his dick entered me. No, I'm sure of it.

"Open your eyes."

My lashes fluttered open, and though I heard him, the next crashing beat was my heart against my sternum.

"Have you changed your mind?"

"No!"

He added pressure to his grind.

"Are you sure?"

"Yes." I grabbed his chiseled, cut hips and pulled him forward, then yelped with every inch he gained.

"Oooooooh!"

"Relax," he murmured, applying pressure as he leaned over me, his body hovering over mine, hips undulating like lapping waves. "Take a deep breath, but don't exhale until I tell you to."

I inhaled, and he drove the entire length of his erection to the base of my cervix.

"Ooooooh shiiiiiiiit! Ah! Oh!"

My eyes crossed, and I unintentionally flexed a Kegel, squeezing him repeatedly as if my pussy had a mind of its own.

"Shit!" he barked, slipping a hand around the back of

my head, our mouths crushed together, and he whispered as he kissed me, "Are you trying to break me with this tight little pussy, Penelope?"

I whimpered, the only sound I could form at the moment. He inched backward, drove in deep again, and lifted my left leg over his shoulder for a better angle.

"Hoooooooly mother!"

He churned me, round and round, in and out, digging deep. Pleasurable sensations swathed my body. My toes curled, my ears popped, my breathing was sporadic.

Sex with him was nothing like I'd experienced before. Hot and heavy, deep and dangerous, wanting to slow down while wanting to feel every bit of the pounding he gave.

I adjusted to his size—finally—and when I inched up my right leg, he lifted from my mouth, pressed his palm on the back of my inching thigh, and fucked me hard.

Slap! Slap! Slap!

The sounds of our colliding flesh echoed between us, and his pummeling drove me mad.

"Aaaaaah!" I arched my back. "Oh shit, Dominic! Dominic!"

A guttural moan burst from him, and I gripped his arms, my nails digging into his skin as I took his thrashing.

I was beaten into the mattress, my body jerking with every whack he pounded. My yells and screams became a chorus with his growls and snarls, elevated by our bodies banging and the passion with which we fucked.

Stings between our legs numbed my thighs with each weighty drop into my center. My head rolled, my body trembled, and my orgasm tore through me like a tsunami.

"Ah! Eeeeeeek!"

My nerves heightened as I felt like a live wire. Dominic slipped out of me, pulled me up, and flipped me over. He was driving inside me from behind before I could gather myself. "Who told you to come, goddess?"

"Oh, fuck!"

Slap! Slap! Slap!

Tight fingers gripped my hips as he banged into me, and I fell into the sheets. Grinding his hips, pounding, stretching me from end to end, I took his unruly hammering. My thighs were coated with the mixture of our sex. It only caused us to slip and slide with harder, more palpable plunges that drove me insane.

"Fucccccck! Dominic! Dominic!"

"Do you want me to stop?"

"No! I want you to come!"

Dark laughter belted from him, and his hand slipped around my neck. "Say *please*."

Pound! Pound! Pound! Pound!

He squeezed my throat, and I croaked out. "Pa...pa...pa."

"I can't hear you, goddess." He loosened his grip, and I took in a breath and squealed.

"Hmmmm."

Pat! Pat! Pat! Pat!

144

"That doesn't sound like *please* to me."

His hot mouth pressed against the back of my shoulders, his hips grinding and undulating.

Dominic was right. I had ample time to say *please*, but I could admit our sex was so intensely driven I didn't want him to stop while at the same time, I did.

"Aaaaah!"

I felt like a madwoman. *What was wrong with me...*

"None of that sounds like please, goddess."

Dominic balanced himself on his hands and rotated his hips, pounding me repeatedly.

"Eeeeeeeeeek! Fuck! Fuck! Fuck! Okay! Okay! Please!"

He withdrew, and I felt his hot come as it splashed my back and coated my ass.

"Uh! Grgggggggh!"

I stuffed my face in the sheets, but I felt like I was floating, my body stinging and heart banging.

There was no way sex like this existed—perhaps I was unaware. Or maybe it was just Dominic, but a girl could wishfully think our coupling drove our passion into fireworks.

I made up my mind that I never wanted to fuck another soul. It was him and him only. It made sense to me, even though technically, this was a trip with my professor, even though society said we were forbidden to indulge like this with one another.

I could never go back. He'd sealed me—added his imprint to my body in a way that it would always be his.

"Dominic, Dominic, Dominic," I mumbled. Slumber heavily taunted me, but I wanted to feel his flesh against mine, wanted him to cuddle me like he loved me and never wanted to let go.

What would I do if he didn't feel the same way? How could I move on from this? From us?

I groaned at the thought, and before I could thoroughly entertain those wicked musings, Dominic's arms covered me, lifted, and I was taken.

WARM WATER COCOONED me in an embrace.

It wasn't the coupling I wanted from Dominic since he'd put me in the bathtub and given me space, but still, the waters were therapeutic, so I accepted it, nonetheless.

I hoped when he came back for me, I wouldn't have drowned because there was no way I could stay awake.

I fought it a little, and I mean a minuscule amount, before drifting off.

15

Dominic

Three days later

The helicopter touched down, making a soft landing. I exited the palace, strolled through the gardens, and climbed inside, seeing Bruno for the first time in a few months.

I carried my eyes over him. In standard fashion he was dressed in black and maroon; slacks, a button-down shirt, a vest, and a wool coat covering his shoulders.

Bruno had been around long enough to be one of the most trustworthy men in the Lucas Cosa Nostra. It's why he was a leader, with capos underneath him.

In age, there was a distance of fifteen years between us. Bruno knew me when I was a boy and watched me grow into the man I am now. He like a lot of capos at the time witnessed Dameon force me into his lifestyle. They saw me challenge it and Bruno witnessed me break and give in. Bruno understood my plight and would pull me to the side on many occasions to check on me and make sure I was thriving mentally. I always gave him a nod or responded with few words until one day I let him in on my frustrations.

I waited for our conversation to be brought up by Dameon. None of the leaders or capos would keep our exchanges away from him. But Bruno had, and for that, I was grateful. Because of this, I allied with him rather than Dameon.

And even though he was one of the few leaders I felt I could trust, my instability to give another human one hundred percent benefit of the doubt made me keep my eye on him, too.

His mouth broke into a smile. "Dominic!" His voice was rough, like he'd smoked a million cigars throughout his life. *"It's good to see you! Are we going inside?"*

He rarely spoke in English. Our conversation went on in Italian. *"Wipe that big-ass silly grin off your face, Bruno, what's gotten into you?"*

He laughed as I smirked. *"You need to smile more often,"* he said. *"It'll do you some good. Make you live longer!"*

"Who told you that shit?"

More laughter shot from him. *"You got a woman I don't know about? Only women make you goofy as fuck."*

"How would you know?"

"Because I do, motherfucker."

He howled, and I shook my head.

"So maybe I do. You should try getting one, and I don't mean anyone, a woman that loves you, eh?"

"You can't trust women, Bruno, you know that. What's gotten into you?"

"I used to believe that bullshit. But I'm telling you, the right one will keep your heart beating long into our dark nights, huh?"

I sucked my teeth and stared at him. I was internally fighting this strange adoration I had for Penelope. And this motherfucker wasn't making it easy.

"How are operations here?"

"Operations are fine. I run a tight ship. My capos don't fuck up like the rumors I've heard about the capos back in New York City."

"Yeah? What have you heard?"

"The Black Rose." His face tightened; jaw locked. *"Whoever this fucker is, he's wreaking havoc, and I don't understand why we haven't killed this son of a bitch."*

I nodded. "Soon."

"That's what I keep hearing, but this guy disappears, then reappears periodically like some fuckin' ghost. We've got to get a handle on this."

"Do you have a plan?"

"Maybe."

"Do you?"

"No."

"No?"

"You can't confront a ghost; the only way to bring him out of the shadows is to have something he wants. Until we know what that is, I plan to protect those around me. Ghost or goblin, no one can get past me."

He nodded, smirked, then slapped me on the back.

"That's the truth. I'm proud of you. You've made one helluva underboss. I always knew you would."

"Yeah, yeah, don't get sentimental on me."

"I will if I want to, damn it."

I glared at him, and he laughed. *"Why are we talking in the helicopter? You hiding something in there?"*

I sucked my teeth again. *"There's a woman inside."*

"A woman?" He perked up.

"Don't get excited."

"Why? You've never given a damn about a woman enough to bring her here, of all places."

"Now you're in my business."

His eyes widened, and he went on a tirade, speed-talking as I watched him. When he calmed and his speech slowed, I responded.

"Are you done?"

"Your business is my business, remember?"

"When I said that, I meant the business of this business. Not my personal business."

"*Excuse me, I didn't know you had personal business, motherfucker.*"

I suppressed a smile. "*She's a friend.*"

"*Oh.*"

"*Only a friend.*"

"*You can't lie to me with a straight face.*"

I sighed deeply. "*She's a friend I like. Are you happy?*" I interrupted him before he responded. "*If not, too fuckin' bad. You'll have to deal with it.*"

He laughed. "*I'm happy for you.*"

"*I'm not getting married, Bruno.*"

"*Maybe. But this is a step.*"

"*You didn't tell me your plan for capturing The Black Rose.*"

He smirked, catching my change of subject, and then his face turned stoic.

"*He's got a pattern.*"

"*Which is?*"

"*He's marking people associated with the business. Those who hold power and the ones between. I think he's vexed. There's something he wanted that he didn't get, and he's pissed about it. I have a feeling it's us, The Lucas Cosa Nostra, who has pissed him off.*"

"*And you think that because...?*"

"*He uses our signature to mark the deaths. It puts us under the gun. Our allies, while maintaining cordial relations with us, look at us with hesitancy now. Their security is deeper and more thorough, and some have refused to share drop points until the last minute."*

"They're wary of us."

"Because they think one of us is The Black Rose." He shook his head. *"How fuckin' insane is that?"*

"With the points you've made, I can see why. It must be why I received looks of indifference at the Niccolò masquerade ball."

"You attended that?"

"I did."

"Why?"

"To represent us and our loyalty to our allies."

He nodded. *"You're smart. I've always liked that about you. Tell me about these looks of indifference."*

"I sensed them coming mainly from Riccardo himself. He's been an annoyance of mine since I was a boy. But this seemed different, a bit tenser than normal. Whenever I caught his eye, there was something more there that I couldn't put my finger on."

"He doesn't trust us."

"If that's the case, then why keep up the charade of being allies?"

"Imagine another family telling us directly that they don't trust us and won't deal with us anymore. That would start a war."

"And nobody wants to go to war with Lucas Cosa Nostra."

"Exactly that."

"*That still doesn't explain how you plan to lure out The Black Rose.*"

"*I've got eyes on all my guys. If it was one of them, I would know.*"

"*Everybody says that—even Rolando, and his capos let their guard down and The Black Rose got to Gianni.*"

His eyes widened and he spit out a slew of profanity.

"*Gianni will be fine, but he's beaten pretty badly, and the priest was killed.*"

"*I saw that on the news and put everyone on high alert.*" He shook his head. "*So that's how it happened.*"

"*Unfortunately. I'm here to give Rolando a chance to fix things with Dameon.*"

"*He's your father, Dominic.*"

"*His name is fuckin' Dameon, isn't it?*"

We stared at each other, and Bruno knew not to push me.

He nodded. "*Don't call him that shit in front of the others.*"

"*Thank you, genius.*"

He glared and I glared back. "*As I said, if The Black Rose is one of us, it isn't one of mine. I've watched their whereabouts for the last few months. When The Black Rose strikes, their movements are accounted for, which means it's no one under my watch.*"

I nodded. "*That's smart, but it could take years to put eyes on everyone in the Lucas Cosa Nostra.*"

"*Yes. But what other choice do we have? We either*

spend years running in circles with our tails tucked between our fuckin' legs or... enact the process of elimination."

I nodded and looked beyond the garden to the house where I saw Penelope looking out the bathroom window. My dick jerked. That was happening more often now that I'd been inside her. Over the last few days, I'd fucked her relentlessly and she'd welcomed it like a starved fiend.

"What does you coming here have to do with Rolando? Can you two not reside in the same city?"

"There's tension."

"Why?"

"You know why."

"Argh! He wants to be in control so bad."

I nodded. *"It'll never happen. Dameon needs to get rid of him."*

Bruno's eyes widened. *"Good luck with that happening."*

"It can be done."

He stared at me in silence and neither one of us spoke for a few minutes.

"Dominic."

"Bruno."

"I don't like where this train of thought is going."

"Don't worry about it. It's my problem to bear."

"Dominic. You know I'm on your side. I trust you. But be careful and if you need someone for anything..."

"I know."

He drew me in a tight embrace and kissed my forehead. I pushed him, opened the helicopter, and stepped out. The blade whipped as the helicopter took flight and I watched him fly off.

Then I went after Penelope.

———

STANDING IN THE DOORWAY, I watched Penelope's silhouette move behind the clear glass shower door. She turned and dropped her head back, letting the spray run over her face and hair down her body. She turned again and spotted me watching.

The door slid open, revealing the goddess she was. I burned like a furnace. That was becoming a regular thing with her.

Slipping out of my shoes, I dropped a trail of clothes on my way inside the stall. The floor would be soaking wet when we exited because I couldn't be bothered with closing the shower door behind me.

Instead, I grabbed her, and she slipped her arms around my neck, her legs around my waist, and I pushed my dick inside her, pressing through her tight, hot pussy.

"I've decided this is the best pussy I've ever had," I murmured in Italian.

Her eyes widened, and she moaned, purring, "Did you just say what I think you said?"

I tightened the grip on her ass, spread her pussy from below, and stroked her against the shower wall.

"Aaaah! Oooooh! Uh!"

Her body vibrated, and I drowned in her pleasure.

"I'm sure of it," I responded, pushing her against my dick as I slammed forward.

"Ah! Oh my, Dominic!"

"Mmmmmm, goddess." I covered her mouth and sucked her tongue as I pummeled her slippery wet pussy.

Slap! Slap! Slap!

My penetration was deep, surging, and passionate. Penelope kissed me with fervor, and our sex exploded like it had many times before.

"Argh! Fuck!" I shouted, digging my grip into her, spanking her pussy repeatedly.

"Shit! Shit! Shit! Ah! Dominic! Yeah! Yes!"

Sounds of wet flesh colliding and a chorus of hails surrounded us as we fucked spiritedly.

"Shiiiiiit! I'm going to come! Now!"

Wet heat covered the entire length of me, and I dropped my lips from her mouth to her nipples.

One after the other, I sucked her perky areolas, continuing my drive as she gripped my shoulders, drew blood with her nails, and writhed against the wall.

I would indeed have a trail of cuts across my shoulders when our time here was over. But it wasn't something I cared about enough to make a difference. If Penelope needed to claw my chest open, I'd let her, as long as she could take this cock in the process.

"Dominic!"

Spank! Spank! Spank! Spank!

I couldn't get enough of Penelope. But most importantly, I never wanted to have my fill of her. It was the first time I'd wanted to keep a woman, which made Penelope a danger to my entire mission in life.

16

Penelope

T had been living a dream. Strangely enough, getting fucked by Dominic day in and out was the thing made of erotic hallucinations. He was a master at everything he did—right down to how he sucked my pussy and made me cream.

I smiled at him sitting across the table. It was our last night here. Tomorrow, reality would resume its bland nature of evolution by comparison. If I had the power to pause time, I would do it now. What girl would ever want to move away from the luxury of this week? Not me. Not anyone.

"You know, I never got to see you dance."

A lone brow rose up his face. "Excuse me?"

"You heard me loud and clear. You didn't do much dancing when we were at the masquerade ball. We spent the night mingling, sipping champagne, and offering polite smiles."

He mused and nodded. "What is your point, goddess?"

He knew calling me goddess aroused me. It was as if he couldn't get enough of me either.

"My point is, you owe me a dance."

He frowned. "I don't recall promising a dance."

"Taking a girl to a ball is promising a dance."

He shook his hand. "Is that what they call girl math?"

I laughed, tickled from end to end. "If it works, then yes."

"I'll turn on some music, and we can dance."

"Nope. That's not good enough."

He rolled in his bottom lip and bit it. "Okay. What would suffice?"

"Take me to a club. Let's go find a club atmosphere, like a party, and let me see you move."

"Penelope, haven't you gotten enough of my movements?"

Heat spilled down my skin, and I leaned forward. "I don't think I'll ever get enough, Dominic."

"No?"

"Never."

He smirked. "A nightclub?"

"Yes. I feel like a club in Italy should be checked off my bucket list."

"You're in your twenties. Why do you have a bucket list?"

I shrugged. "I don't. It's a figure of speech. Clubbing in Italy is one of the once-in-a-lifetime things, right?"

"Wrong."

Surprised, I twisted my lips. "Were you born and raised here?"

"Yes."

"Oh. So, then you know all of the great spots, huh?"

"Were you born and raised in the States?"

"Yes, but my parents made sure I learned to speak Italian early on. They spoke it in the home but everywhere else, English."

"I see." He checked his watch. "We leave in the morning to go back to New York. Do you think you can handle a night out tonight?"

"Yes."

"You've got one hour to be ready to fly to the city."

I left the table in a rush, showered quickly, and added depth to my wavy hair with the hot curling wand I'd packed in my luggage. I kept watch on the time, wanting to be prompt but ensuring I covered my bases. I brushed my teeth, flossed, and brushed my tongue for the second time.

After applying body butter, I withdrew two clothing options for tonight.

One was a body-hugging one-piece, see-through pantsuit. It teased the eye by barely showing my panties and bra underneath. It was hot for sure, but I wanted to make it easy for Dominic to fuck me as he wished if the opportunity presented itself.

So, with that in mind, I selected the thigh-high cocktail dress. I would freeze my ass off wearing this, but if Dominic brought the heat...oh, it would be worth it.

I giggled and slipped into the cocktail dress, slid three-inch-high heels on my feet, and added my costume jewelry.

Three deep sprays of Tom Ford's Lost Cherry had me smelling like expensive fruit; the kind that was rare and worth a million bucks.

I was ready, leaving the bedroom just in time. My heels echoed off the Italian tile floors as I strutted to the front door, and Dominic turned to look at me. His debonair gaze crawled over me, touching every part of my body like a silky caress.

I tingled just a bit; the magic from his stare warmed me. He walked towards me, my dark knight, covered in his usual black attire from head to toe.

"You're the most beautiful girl in the world, Penelope." He took a finger down the side of my face, and I blushed, and bit the corner of my red lips.

My heart rhythm caught an extra beat, and my blush deepened. "Thank you." My lashes fluttered. "I never met a man as poised as you, Dominic. Has anyone ever told you that you're perfect?"

His lips spread slowly into a smile, his heavy gaze holding me captive as his hands dropped to my thigh and slid to the seat of my panties. "You would take that back if you knew everything about me, goddess."

I quivered as his fingers traced my clit through the fabric, my body reacting to him in a way that told me what I already knew—I belonged to him.

"I don't think I would. I love your dark side, too."

Deep laughter expelled from his gut. "You don't know my dark side, sweetheart."

"Whatever it is, I like it and I can deal with it."

"I may test that theory. Now is the only time to take it back. If you plan to stay around, that is."

"You mean, if you plan to keep me around."

He tilted his head. "Or that."

He waited for me to take it back, but I kept my lips closed. Dominic sucked his teeth. "Have it your way."

Removing his hand from my clit, that same finger lifted my chin, and he placed a hot kiss on my mouth.

When he lifted from my lips, our breaths rushed between each other, and I was lost in his gaze when his fingers snapped, and he ordered:

"Jacket."

A server came from nowhere with an ankle-length wool coat and slipped it over my shoulders.

"Shall we?"

"Yes."

THE FULL MOON was a silvery sphere in the dark night sky, and I imagined if we were werewolves, it would have activated our transformation. We glided down the dark streets in Dominic's luxury vehicle – passing classical and renaissance buildings that transported the city's nightlife.

As frigid as it was outside, inside the Lexus, I was sheltered in a calming warmth that blasted from the vents but also emanated from Dominic and me.

Much like when we road his motorcycle back in New York, Dominic didn't obey the rules of the road, cutting down side streets, blowing past red lights, ditching Italian authorities, and zigzagging around people walking the roads.

I gripped the door handles tight and screamed every time I thought he would run someone or something over while he laughed.

He seemed to get a kick out of scaring the wits out of me. But I was down for the ride.

Why?

While Dominic was a bit unhinged, there were layers that I'd been privy to. I had witnessed, this calm, well-collected side of him that rarely spoke, brooded often, was observant, and only made moves when the move was necessary; calculated, even. Each decision he made had a purpose that only he knew about. I felt drawn to that hidden side of him.

Another layer of him was the devil dressed in Armani. Intensely dark and ominous, so much so that it wouldn't surprise me if he could kill a man and walk away as if he didn't just take a life. I shuddered at the thought of that part of him.

While I wasn't one hundred percent sure he was a killer, the times he'd revealed that part to me always made me run. It was a shift. His demeanor frosted over, and he went cold; that calm side that I'd come to love disappeared like he'd sucked his own soul away and replaced it with something otherworldly.

He didn't see me for me then. Because he had been replaced by this thing of ominous nature—except that it was also him. The alternate Dominic would arrive and shake my core, then disappear, almost like he'd gotten his point across.

The calm part of him could control it; at least, that was what I thought—or more likely, what I hoped.

We arrived at a medieval Roman-like structure and parked in a garage next to tall columns.

At the elevator, we rode silently to the fifteenth floor, and he entered a code on the keypad for the doors to open.

Alternative music blasted as we stepped off and walked into the throngs of people dancing. It seemed as if we exited in the middle of the dance floor with people shaking their hips, multicolored lights hovering over us, and aerial dancers swinging from the ceiling.

Dominic grabbed my hand and twirled me right into his embrace. My hands landed on his chest, and a smile curved my lips.

Our hips moved in sync, rotated to the beat of the music. His hands carried over my waist, gripped me there, and held me full against the bulge in his pants.

Aroused instantly, I pushed back into his pelvis, feeling his firm heat against my stomach, and suddenly wished I could suck him off right then and there.

His steps matched mine, completely in sync with each other, no missteps between us. I was surprised by his smooth moves, heightened by his skill, and stimulated by his touch.

A caress on my elbows, a grip on my hips, feather kisses on my face, and neck, grips on my ass. I moaned and squirmed, lost in erotic sensation, my body completely aware and showered with heat by the second.

"Oooh, I could stay here with you forever."

"Why would you want to do that?" his deep voice purred.

"Because you're my equal."

That dangerously dark guffaw spilled from his mouth. "Penelope, Penelope..." he drawled.

"You act like I'm wrong, but look how well we match."

He held me tight, licked his lips, and grinned. "We don't match, we get along."

"I think you're wrong."

"You've been quite insistent on this."

"That's because if we were not, I would've been repulsed by you from the moment you choked me out in your office."

More dark laughter fell from him. "I remember you running away. What do you remember?"

"I wouldn't call it running per se, more like...getting my bearings."

More laughter sprang from his lips. His gaze lit up, then darkened as he shook his head. "You are quite the storyteller, Penelope."

"Except the only story I'm telling is our truth."

He stared at me, his gaze level. Dominic twirled me around slowly, then cupped me under his arm, wrapping that arm around my shoulders. "Let me show you something."

We strolled off the dance floor, climbed a metal staircase, and walked to a door at the end.

A sign above it read *NO EXIT*, but he put his foot in the middle and kicked it open.

Cold air blasted across my face, my hair whirling as we stepped onto the rooftop.

"For that door to be labeled *NO EXIT*, whoever the owner is, didn't make it difficult to break through."

"We were watched. But no one will stop me."

"You're a regular?"

"I grew up here, but that is not the reason no one will stop me."

"He didn't elaborate, and I didn't ask for clarification." I pulled my hair from my face and caught the view of the Leaning Tower of Pisa. It was large and appeared close with lights that sparkled and blinked like a beautiful constellation of stars.

"Wow. That's probably the most amazing thing I've ever seen."

Dominic tightened his hold on me. "We should get closer. At the edge, it feels like you can reach out and touch it."

We strolled to the roof's edge, and I couldn't help but notice no safety rail or brick lining the sides were in place.

"This is pretty dangerous," I said, more focused on the drop below than the tower.

"Yes," he drawled. "It's why the owners don't want anyone out here."

I shivered, and he removed his arm, and immediately I felt the full force of the cold winds, pushing me like a bully on a high school playground.

"Oh!" I stepped forward, slipped, and tried to gain my footing but failed. "Ooh!"

A scream yanked through my throat as I fell over the edge but was caught by the spikey ledge ripping through my coat's fabric.

It felt like I swallowed my heart, panic surged through me, and I turned my eyes up at Dominic to see him standing idly on that same edge, watching me with no rush to help save me from a life-threatening dilemma.

"Dominic!" I screamed, and that's when I saw him—the otherworldly part of him was there, and I froze, realizing I might not make it out of this alive.

My heart ricocheted, and even in the frosty weather, sweat beaded across my forehead, behind my ears, and between my breasts.

"Please," I begged as the thread in my coat ripped a little more, dropping me another inch, a fair warning that I was minutes or maybe seconds away from gravity taking hold and spreading me along the ground like salsa.

"Do you still love my dark side, Penelope?"

When he'd said my name this time, only fear struck my core, but that wasn't the scariest thing at the moment.

"You won't let me fall. You won't!" I shrieked, hanging over the edge of a damn building like a lunatic. It was that single moment that told me, girl, you are technically already falling.

My stomach bubbled and then constricted.

Another rip in my coat, another inching drop and I closed my eyes and thought of my life, my friends, my parents, and what I had made of myself.

My breathing steadied. If this was it, I'd done okay. There was nothing stellar about my time here, but I could reasonably say I'd added happiness to someone's life. My friends, my parents, even my uncle Dexter, who'd only visit me once a month on the weekends when he wasn't at the reserves.

Do you still love my dark side, Penelope?

His ominous question shook me, or maybe he'd repeated it, but it was not likely. The next life could be calm, adventurous, and happy, couldn't it?

My breathing calmed to a regular draw, and I opened my eyes, stared up at Dominic, and breathed, "Yes."

His eyes dilated, jaw locked, head tilted, and my coat ripped. I closed my eyes again, waiting for my descent, when I was snatched up before I could plummet.

My eyes shot open, my hands gripped his shoulders, and the reality of what just happened pushed a gasp from my mouth.

"I don't know," he drawled, still combing me with that heavy-lidded dark gaze. "Maybe we are a match."

He dragged me from the edge, lifted me higher, and I clung to him—arms around his shoulders, legs around his waist.

Our mouths crashed, and we sucked the breath from each other, panting, adrenaline coursing through my veins. Turning, he pushed me into the brick wall of the entrance, ripped my pantyhose, and shoved his dick inside me.

"OOOOH!"

I moaned, quivered, and tightened my legs around him as he pounded me relentlessly. Pleasure consumed us. I bit his mouth drawing blood, and he bit me back, licking away the blood with his tongue. Lips stretched over my chin to my neck, and sucked my throat as he pumped his big, hard cock like a drilling machine.

It was safe to say he was aroused by my almost-fatal

plummet; that, or he believed what I had always known. We were a match, made in heaven or hell or somewhere between.

Still, he knew, and I'd almost died in the process to convince him.

17

Manhattan Excellence & Arts University

Penelope

"Where the hell have you been...and don't you dare lie!"

Pulling from my trance, I looked at Emma with a smile curling up my face. "Why am I getting such a wild accusation thrown my way?"

"I haven't accused you of anything yet."

"You're insisting that I might lie."

"And you're stalling."

I sighed as Alice and Sofia joined us at the cafeteria table. "It's early. Do we have to start the morning this way?"

Alice looked at Emma. "Is she stalling?"

Emma nodded. "She is."

Sofia giggled. "This must be good. Never have you gone completely MIA for an entire week." She wiggled in her seat. "So tell us. Who is he, and did you have mind-numbing sex?"

I laughed out loud. "Leaving my phone was a mistake."

"The first lie," Emma chirped.

I gawked and turned my eyes to her. "Emma."

"Penelope." She angled her head, letting me know she was on to me.

I laughed again and dropped my head on the table, covering my face at the sides. I couldn't lie with a straight face if I wanted to. They all knew it, and even now, as a rush of laughter escaped me, I didn't know why I tried.

I sucked in my amusement and lifted my head. When I did, an image in the background caught my attention.

Standing at a vending machine dressed in Brioni, Dominic reached inside the machine's mouth, his muscular back flexing through the shirt. He removed a bottle of water, twisted the top, and drank, and I watched as a droplet landed on his bottom lip when he pulled the bottle from his mouth.

His head turned, his gaze locking with mine. He winked and strolled away, and every nerve in my body danced wildly.

I'd been fucked by Dominic's dark side, and now I felt different—risky. That was the only way to explain it.

"Ahem!"

I blinked back at Sofia, who was staring at me, waiting for my explanation. Emma, however, was already watching the direction of my attention.

Squinting, she turned back to me. "Are you fucking our professor?"

Gasps shot from Alice and Sofia, their mouths hanging wide.

If anyone could burst my secret open, it would be Emma.

"Sssshush!" My eyes widened, and I scolded her. "Why would you say something like that so loudly?"

She glanced around and whispered. "Sorry. I'm just...well, you've been keeping something from us, and I've felt like I needed to become Nancy Drew to find out."

"Or, or..." I whisper-shouted, "You all could mind your business!"

More gasps, and I rolled my eyes. "Why would you say that to us like we're strange weirdos?"

I pursed my lips and smirked. I knew what came next.

"I thought we were sisters." She laid a hand over her chest, and Sofia followed her lead like clockwork.

"The closest a sister can be without being blood-related," Sofia added.

"Maybe we were wrong," Emma said, her lips sagging like she was hurt.

"I can't take either of you seriously right now."

"And that's what's wrong," Sofia added.

"Listen, I didn't want to say anything until I was sure, okay?"

"Sure of what?" Alice said, finally adding to the conversation.

"That this guy might like me."

"So there is a guy," Sofia said.

"Of course, there's a guy," Emma answered.

Alice's face brightened. "Who is he?"

"And most importantly," Sofia stuck her violet-manicured nail out at me. "Did you have sex while you've been missing in action?"

I smirked. "What is with you and the sex question?"

She pouted. "I must live vicariously through someone because the vibrator is not cutting it."

Laughter lifted from our table, and Emma shook her head. "Poor thing." She rubbed Sofia's back.

"Thanks," Sofia sniffled. She looked back at me, "So?"

"Yes. I had sex."

"I knew it!" Sofia screamed. Emma's mouth dropped, but nothing came out, and Alice clasped her hands together, her eyes wide with intriguing pleasure.

Alice held a hand up, and I high-fived her. "My girl!"

"It was the best sex I've ever had in my life," I added. And as much as I intended to keep Dominic to myself, sharing some of our time together felt good. "In fact," I add, "I'm sure none of you have had sex like this."

Their mouths dropped even further, and I giggled deeply.

"Who is he?" Emma finally said. "Is it the professor?"

"Why do you want it to be him so badly?"

"He's hot. I think you can take him, and he would bite. Also, he was gone for a week, same as you."

My brows rose, and so did Sofia and Alice.

"Are you sure?" Sofia asked, "I thought I saw him twice last week."

Emma frowned. "Are you sure?"

I let them go back and forth, but noticed Alice staring at me with a huge smile.

"You seem overly happy."

She opened her mouth, closed it, and then blurted, "I had sex, too."

Gasps shot from Emma and Sofia, but this time, my mouth hung open. I inwardly thanked Alice for the save. She'd effectively turned the interrogation to her.

"What the actual hell?!" Emma shouted.

Alice and I laughed. Emma squinted at me and pointed. "I'm not done with you, by the way." Her pointing finger switched to Alice. "But you...when did *you* have time to have sex?"

I shook my head and held back a laugh.

Alice twisted her lips. "Hmmmm, when you two were obsessed with finding out where Penelope was."

"We weren't obsessed, just concerned," Emma said.

Sofia nodded. "Totally concerned."

I cracked a smile but didn't say a word. Alice smirked. "Sure you weren't."

"Tell us the details," Emma demanded. "Now. Both of you."

"I think they should go one at a time. I need all the juicy details, and I do mean juice."

Alice laughed while I responded. "Sofia, you're just going to get yourself really horny, and how will you solve that problem?"

"I..." Her mouth closed as she thought about it. "Shit."

We laughed.

"You're not supposed to laugh at my pain."

"We're laughing with you, not at you," Alice said.

"But I'm not laughing."

We glanced at each other and laughed again.

"Ugh! You guys!"

"Well, you could give it up to Barry; he's been giving you the googly-eyes all semester."

"But I want Ethaaaaaan."

"Oh God, here we go again."

"It's not fair!"

"Go on and fuck him then." We all glanced at Alice.

"What?"

A look of hope crossed Sofia's face, and I grimaced. There was no way I could be a part of this train wreck.

"Why would you tell her that?" I asked.

Alice shrugged and flicked an auburn strand of hair behind her ear.

"She wants to get laid and doesn't want to lay with just

anyone. It's understandable. Who are we to stop her from going after who she wants?"

"Her friends," Emma pointed out.

"Yes, yes, but we've told her the consequences about giving Ethan sex, so now it's up to her. And if he breaks her heart—"

"When," I said. "Fixed it for you."

They glanced at each other, and Sofia pouted.

"Oh, for God's sake," I murmured. "Finish, Alice."

"When..." she cleared her throat. "He breaks or if..." she decided, "...cause who knows, he could surprise us all—"

Emma and I groaned, and she hurried to convey her point. "Then we'll deal with it."

"And what will we do?" I asked.

Alice shrugged. "Find her someone new to get under. That's the quickest way to get over a man, right?"

The bell rang, and I was happy to rise from my seat. The conversation had taken an undesirable turn.

"Hey, we still have topics to cover!"

I paused mid-lift. "Yes, but we have to go to class. Let's talk after."

We grabbed our bags and belongings and went in opposite directions.

18

Dominic

One month later

11:36 PM

Vito Cappalli went untouchable for the sixty-one years of his reign because of the high-tech security he kept installed and upgraded year-round. Over the last two years, I'd watched him come and go, but every entrance and exit required codes, retina scans, fingerprint scans, and cameras were installed that covered every inch of his compound.

It could be argued that he was paranoid. But that paranoia had kept him alive because even I hadn't been able to breach his compound – until now.

It took the carelessness of his heir and underboss, Antonio Cappalli, to lend me a view complete with audio recordings of every move they made. The boss and underboss spoke frequently, shared secrets, fucked the same women, and spoke openly about their plans to sell more cocaine than they could handle.

As the underboss of the Lucas Cosa Nostra, I admired their tenacity.

As The Black Rose—I hated the thought of them living through the next day. Antonio Cappalli had given me all I needed. More than enough, actually, and as it turned out, I wouldn't need to penetrate Vito's compound to get to him.

I ordinarily preferred to be in the same room when my mark went down, but for this exercise, I watched from the tiny camera embedded in the food tray that waited for Vito by the bedside, where he fucked his eighty-nine-year-old mother-in-law.

Two stainless steel domed food covers sat on the serving tray. It was Vito's birthday night. Antonio had thrown his father a celebration worthy of a president. All their closest friends and family were there. Mafia families had received invites for an evening of unparalleled festivity.

Vito was on his third bottle of Chateau d'Yquem Sauternes when his mother-in-law, Valentina Cappalli, sauntered up to him and delivered a kiss on his face.

"*Happy Birthday,*" she said. "*You were always my favorite child.*"

"You've said that often, mamma; I think it's time you prove it."

He slapped her ass and drew her in for an open-mouthed kiss that had onlookers exiting the room quickly.

Sixty seconds later, they were naked, their sex escapades spilling from the front room to Vito's quarters, and Victor Cappalli—the former Boss—was none the wiser.

He sat in a room downstairs with an entire caregiving team that wiped the saliva that occasionally dripped down his lips. In a world unknown to him—his memory loss came with a crippling illness that rendered him incapable of understanding who the people were around him or who he, himself, was.

Formerly one of the cruelest mafiosi, Victor had reigned with an iron fist. If anyone made the slightest mistake, he would annihilate one's entire family. Ruling like this made him feared, hated, and most importantly, powerful. In the underworld, power was everything. However, now Victor was a shell of the man he once was, and no amount of that power would reverse the effects of his failing health.

Screams and shouts filled Vito's room as he and Valentina went on like horny teenagers filled with energy they'd waited to release.

Seconds turned into minutes, and just when I thought he'd make me wait a little longer, they fell on top of each other, panting and sweating like animals in the jungle.

"*I should've fucked you sooner,*" Vito said, causing Valentina to laugh.

"*Why didn't you?*"

"*I would think that answer is obvious.*"

She pinched his cheek. "*It's been a long time since your father made any sense. Years. You could've had me a long time ago. Besides, I'm only rotting away at his side. Might as well not let the pussy go to waste, yeah?*"

They laughed together, finding amusement in their sweaty fever.

"*I didn't even get a slice of cake, for fuck's sake.*"

"*Aww, you can get cake anytime. Besides, the chef had some delivered to you.*"

He sat up and looked at the serving tray beside the bed.

At my warehouse, I settled in my chair and kept my eyes locked on the moment I'd been waiting for.

"*So he did,*" Vito said.

He stood up and strolled, bare-ass, to the tray and lifted the right stainless-steel dome.

"*Would you like a bite?*"

She sighed, still floating on cloud nine. "*Sharing?*"

"*I've shared everything else; might as well share a bite of cake.*"

She stood and walked over to him as he grabbed the large slice and put half of it in his mouth. Turning the cake, he stuffed more than she could handle in her mouth, and she laughed and took a step back, choking and clearing her throat as she swallowed.

He nodded and frowned. *"That's...hmmm. The sweetest cake I've ever had."*

Seconds ticked by when he lifted the second dome to find a single long-stemmed black rose.

His eyes widened, immediately aware of its symbolism. When he grabbed his throat, I knew it was tightening as the cyanide began to close off his oxygen.

His body jerked, and he flailed, and just as swiftly, Valentina began coughing in response to her lethal bite.

They fell to the ground, gasping, flipping like fishes out of water, while Vito tried to grab the cell phone lying on the night table with all his might. Veins bulged from his face, and he braced himself for what he knew would inevitably come next.

Of all the precautions he'd taken through the years—even going so far as to make his chef taste the food he made for him before he ate it—this night, birthday night, Vito loosened enough to give me an inch, and it was all I needed to take him out of the picture.

The black rose would shake the foundation of the Cappalli familia, and try as he might, Antonio's fate was sealed.

I KEPT TO MY ROUTINE: I changed my clothes, stuffed them in a duffle bag, and pushed them into an incinerator to be discarded.

Back at home, I showered, pulled a beer from the fridge, and lit a cigar while I mused over the night's success. My thoughts, however, were jumbled where I used to be clear-minded. What I wanted was to be under Penelope—inside her, where wild passion and pleasure consumed me, filled me, and shifted me into something whole.

I pulled deeply on my cigar and exhaled through my nose as I mused. Over the last month, I'd been absorbed in Vito Cappalli and Penelope Cattaneo. Navigating the two worlds was like night and day, but what I noticed was being heavily consumed by both gave me balance.

That balance kept my anger grounded instead of on edge like before. Whereas something as simple as watching people going about their everyday happy lives would enrage me, now it didn't. The stress ball I kept in my pockets had been in my office drawer at the school for weeks, and I'd yet to reach for it to use it.

I was changing. The balance that kept me even had changed me, and I knew that came from my close proximity to Penelope.

She thought we were a match. And I'd come to believe her, but not in the way that she assumed.

Penelope was my anchor, and I'd yet to figure out what it was that I provided her beside this heavily erected cock.

Beep.

I glanced down, removed my second cell phone, and swiped at the notification that opened one of the four mini-cameras I had set up in Penelope's home. They were motion-sensor activated, giving me a view of her whenever I desired it. I'd set these up the night the thunderstorm kept her shivering underneath the covers until I'd put her to sleep with my tongue.

My dick hardened thinking about it, and I watched her, clad in a thong, sleepwalk to the refrigerator, and return to her bed seconds later.

She plopped across the sheets, falling back into slumber before pulling herself underneath the duvet. I watched her for five minutes, ten, and fifteen, and she lifted her head, reached for her cell phone, and checked to see if she'd received anything from me.

I smirked. I'd yet to give Penelope a number to contact me. She didn't need it. When she wanted me, I arrived. When I wanted her, I watched until the strain in my dick couldn't take watching any longer, and I went after her.

Like now.

The door slammed behind me as I left my house in Corniquea Hills and drove across town. When I pulled onto her street, I went around the block three times, sweeping the area before I pulled into her driveway. On the front porch, I removed the spare key she had hidden under a plant and let myself inside.

I'd long since taught myself how to move through a

space without sound. I did that now, entered Penelope's room, removed my boots and jeans, and dropped my shirt to the floor.

At her bedside, I slipped the covers back and wrapped my arms around her, drawing her body close and shifting us underneath the duvet.

Her arms snaked around my neck, and her legs wrapped around my waist.

"I thought you'd never come," she murmured, half-asleep.

"You should know better than that by now," I said, moving her panties to the side.

Adjusting my dick, I stuck my cock inside her, and her body arched as a moan dropped from her lips.

Fully awake, Penelope's eyes opened, and she smiled at me as I sucked in her tongue.

"Mmmmmmmmmm."

Her legs tightened around my waist, and I dipped and ground inside her. She had the wettest pussy I'd ever had. Tight as a motherfucker, and elite on every level. I could fuck her into the next century and never tire of her.

I bit down her chin, sucked her neck, and dropped my mouth to her nipples.

"Ooooh..." her hips bucked, her body stretched, and a quiver swept over her as I churned her tight pussy. "Yesssss, oh, more, *more*..."

I gave her what she asked for, heavy strokes that

elicited purrs and moans that turned into screams of passion.

She drove me crazy in a way that made me sane.

It was something I never saw happening to me. My life had been consumed by this raging fire within me. Inherently, the effect turned me into The Black Rose, and my only mission in life had been that one.

But Penelope reminded me what I'd wanted all along for myself – a life of normalcy, laughter, joy, and passion unadulterated.

———————

"YOU WILL DO *what you're supposed to do. From here on out, I don't want to hear you mention doing your own thing. Or becoming some do-gooder. You will stand by my side, learn from me, carry out my demands, and bed the women needed to get next to an enemy if that is what is required of you.*"

My father's words reverberated in my head, clashing with the bliss my mind tried to remind me of. His proclamation came at a time when I fought him on being the heir to his criminal throne—when I stood for myself and was determined to be different than him.

He'd snatched the option from my hands like a wicked thief, tricking me into believing his life was in danger. I killed a man because of it. Still in my teens and shocked to my core, I was horrified.

He laughed at my expression, and mocked my words. The blood was on my hands now. There was no turning back, and that was enough to turn me into The Black Rose.

"YOU WILL DO *what you're supposed to do.*" His words repeated.

———

I PUMPED INTO PENELOPE, my thrusts more powerful than before. The bed rocked, her moans louder, her fingers tightly digging into my back.

"OH! OH! OH!"

With each pound, she yelped—with each grind, she trembled.

"Fuck! Fuck! Fuck!" she screamed, and I snarled and emptied come inside her, my body shaking as I howled, ignited like I'd been set on fire.

"Oooooh!" Her chest rose and fell, her gasps heavy as she rushed to catch her breath. "You're so intense when you fuck!"

Her words were a mix of Italian and French, and the mix made me want to straighten her language and give her tips on how to keep her words steady.

She moaned as I removed myself from her, but I

turned Penelope in my arms and curled beside her before she began to shiver.

She was...always cold until she was with me, and she'd shiver uncontrollably anytime we disconnected.

Her body undulated as she pushed her ass against me, snuggled under my chin, and didn't waste time drifting off to sleep.

19

Dominic

Casinò di Lucas

"Well, my brother finally visits me."

I waited until the door behind me shut before I addressed my sister, Luna. I swept my eyes around the security room, where she had made her official office.

"You said that as if I'm a long-lost sibling."

"Might as well be. Where have you been, and more importantly, what have you been doing?"

"I was out of the country for a week and busy cleaning up behind Rolando before that."

She nodded. "And after?"

"Busy."

"Of course. So, like I said, you might as well be a long-lost sibling."

I strolled to her and sat in a chair beside hers. "Do you miss me, sister?"

"If I did, I wouldn't tell you."

I cracked a smile. "That tells me enough."

I glanced at the monitors—two hundred and thirties cameras covered every angle, direction, and inch of the place. Nothing slipped past Luna.

"You need to take a break."

Her raven-black hair swayed across her shoulder when she shook her head. "Not happening."

"You must trust someone other than yourself to do this job."

"Do you?"

"What?"

"Do you trust someone other than yourself to handle your job as the underboss?"

I stared back at eyes similar to mine, and she waited patiently for a response she already knew the answer to.

"Exactly," she answered.

"That's a totally different scenario." I shook my head.

"Why? Because your job is more important than mine?"

"Yes."

She reared back, eyes wide, and I dropped my head and laughed. She pushed me as I howled, the moment making me miss our back-and-forth.

"You came here to get on my damn nerves, didn't you?"

I reined in my laughter. "Didn't you just accuse me of being a lost sibling? Now, I can't get on your nerves a little bit?"

She rolled her eyes and crossed her legs. "Why are you cleaning up after Rolando?"

I leaned back in the chair and stared at her momentarily, then caught her up on what had happened. She shook her head and sighed. "It's unlike him to be that sloppy."

"Because he can't keep his eyes off me."

Her brows arched in surprise, then she frowned. "What do you mean?"

"He wants to be the only one to get in Dameon's ear."

"You mean our father?"

We stared at each other. "Must we go through this every time he's brought up?"

"Yes, I will. You know how this works."

I closed my mouth and gritted my teeth.

As much as my sister loved me, she loved Dameon just as much. And she wanted us to be that father-and-son duo I pretended to be.

Still, she understood how my madness had stirred throughout the years. She just didn't know how far down the rabbit hole I'd gone to get my payback.

"Rolando is power-hungry."

Her frown deepened. "Should I be worried?"

"We all should be."

"Have you told our father how you feel?"

"No."

"Why? He'll listen to you."

"He will want us to find a way to come together. He will think we can 'fix' our issues when it's not an issue of mine at all. Rolando needs to go."

Her eyes widened, and she sighed. "Damn it, Dominic."

"He does."

"Change the subject."

"Mark my words."

She eyed me in silence, then glanced at the screen. "Who's the blonde bombshell with you?"

Her switch in the topic was smooth but not slick.

"She isn't blonde."

"Looks blonde to me."

"Then you should get your eyes fixed."

A slow smile crept across her lips. "Damn, brother. Are you offended?"

"Are you blind?"

"According to you." She sniffed. "Who is she?"

"A student."

She glanced between me and the monitor, where she watched Penelope play a game of blackjack.

"You're fucking your students now?"

"Who said I was fuckin' anyone?"

"Are you?"

"Since when do you want to talk about my sex life?"

"Since you started fuckin' your students."

I smirked and shook my head, inhaling. "It's a rare case, trust me."

"I believe you, but why risk your career over a lay when you can have anyone you want?"

A guffaw belted from me. "My career?" I sniped.

"What's so off-putting about what I said?" She drew herself up, indignant.

"No one can ruin me. You'll do well to remember that, sister."

"Oh yes, I almost forgot," she teased.

"Besides, it's a farce of a position anyway."

"Did you not graduate from school and have the degrees for the position?"

"You know what the fuck I mean," I barked, annoyed that she'd decided to fuck with me.

"You could put your focus on your position and give up some of your duties in the Cosa Nostra. You're the underboss; assign your responsibilities to someone else and live the life you've always wanted."

I shook my head and stood.

"Where are you going?"

"Away from you." I turned to leave.

"Wait a minute, that's all I get? Fifteen, almost twenty lousy minutes?"

"You've obviously lost your mind. There's no talking to a crazy person."

"How is it crazy for me to offer you a suggestion?"

I turned back to Luna, eyes wide, "The fuckery you're speaking of would never work. Dameon would see to it that I remain just as I am. Trust me!" I yelled. "But two, I've gone much too far over the deep end to pretend to have a normal life for the sake of fulfilling a fairy tale I'll never have."

"Okay." She nodded. "I understand. Seriously."

We watched each other for a minute, and I exhaled harshly.

"Luna, don't mention it again."

"I won't."

The cell phone I used for calls only from Dameon buzzed. I removed it and glanced at a text message.

Meet me at the estate now.

I frowned and wondered what could be of such utter importance.

"What's that look?"

"Dameon wants me to meet him."

"Sounds important."

I sucked my teeth. "Could be more Rolando bullshit."

"Does he know about her?"

I glanced from my phone to Luna. "What is there to know?"

"That you like a girl, maybe even got a crush."

"What the fuck are you talking about?"

"Don't bullshit me, Dominic. You've never brought a woman here. She was the same one from the Billiards Club. It's been a few months. Seems pretty serious."

"How the fuck do you know about the Billiards Club?"

"Do you even have to ask that? I see all things."

"Because you're constantly watching security cameras and tapes, what good will it do you?"

"There's been no one killed by The Black Rose on my watch."

It was an accolade for her as it was with Bruno, and she was right. They both were. But that was because I genuinely loved them, and spilling blood under their watch never crossed my mind.

"Touché." I slipped my phone in my pocket. "And no, he doesn't and won't know about her, will he, Luna?"

"Not unless he demands to go over the recordings."

"And when does he ever do that?"

"So far, he hasn't done it in decades, but he also hasn't had a reason to. He may order it if we don't stop The Black Rose."

"We?"

"Yes, Dominic, me and you. I feel if we work together, we can stop him."

"Him?"

"Whatever the fuck it is."

I smirked. "I'll talk to you later, sister." I turned to exit. "Oh, her name is Penelope. She wants to meet you."

"What does she know about me?"

"That you're my badass, annoying little sister."

She twisted her lips. "Get out, Dominic."

I laughed. "Do me a favor and go meet her, and while you're at it, tell her I had an emergency and offer her a ride home."

"Damn, you really do like her, don't you?"

I left without responding, but Luna's laughter haunted me down the halls.

20

Dominic

"It's time."

Dameon closed the door to his study and walked back to his desk, where I stood. He gripped me on the shoulder, and we eyed each other.

"Give me the details," I said.

He strolled to the cigar cabinet and removed pre-cut cigars. After lighting two, he handed me one and poured me a short glass of liquor.

Dameon strolled to the window and stared out at the horizon. "Our allies are increasingly spooked by this Black Rose son of a bitch. I've been in touch with Bruno, and you were right. He's on top of shit like we should be here."

"So what's the plan?"

He turned to look at me. "The entire underworld is whispering, Dominic, and the things they say have our allies looking at us with indifference."

"Who? Point them out, and I will strike them down."

He smirked. "I'm proud of you. If I've never told you that, understand that you're my pride and joy." He paused, his mind musing. "I know we had a rough start," he mumbled. It was the closest he'd come to saying anything about my youth. "But we've put it behind us, and you've become the spitting image of me with the moves you make."

That only angered me. And in that singular moment, I wished I had my stress ball.

"Continue to make me proud. I know you will."

"Of course, Father."

He nodded and his lips thinned. "It's time, Dominic. In just under a few months, you'll marry into the Cappalli family to tie our family bonds and strengthen our relationships. It's the only thing that matters now."

Surprise rippled through me, and with it, the anger I felt clouded my vision and drummed against my skull, giving me an instant massive headache.

"How does that help our current situation?"

"You don't understand how powerful you are, son. You've made a name for yourself in the underworld. Having you as a son-in-law guarantees safety. No one is willing to come against you or me. Therefore, we must reassure our friends and link with two of the most powerful families next to ours—the Cappallis and the Niccolòs."

I locked my jaw and kept my breathing steady. I knew

this day would one day come, but to know I was the reason to usher it in must have been a bit of my karma swinging at me tenfold.

"We? You mean me. How will we link with the both of them?"

"I also mean me, too."

Surprised, a deep guffaw dropped from my mouth, but Dameon's serious demeanor sucked that mirth from my gut straightaway.

"That is not a joke?"

"Why would it be?"

"You're sixty-nine fuckin'-years old."

He frowned and glared. "And still breathing. My dick still gets hard. What does my age have to do with it?"

I reined in my annoyance and straightened my shoulders. "I didn't think you would wed again."

His glare dropped, and he inhaled a deep breath. "You mean after your mother."

I locked my jaw. I never talked about my mother. She was a ghost who abandoned me as soon as I'd arrived, so there was no point.

"Yes, well, that was the plan, but plans change, and right now, this is the only thing that matters." He took a sip of his liquor.

"Drink up. In the next coming weeks, things will move fast."

I swallowed the entire glass in a single gulp, slammed it on the desk, and nodded. "As you wish."

Drawing on the cigar, I turned my back and left the office, needing to blow off some steam.

Philadelphia, Pennsylvania

LIGHTNING SCATTERED ACROSS THE SKY, followed by rumbles of thunder. I found it appropriate that the weather aligned with my mood—hostile and violent.

After changing at the warehouse, I'd asked myself why anger fired through me with untethered vehemence. What did I stand to lose in a life where my existence wasn't living in the first place?

But I knew the answer, even though I tried to deny it. I would lose the one person who had given me purpose and shared the only joy I'd ever felt in a world so cold.

Penelope.

I'd rather cut my own head off before marrying into the Cappalli family. But before I set the time and date for my own demise, I would kill everyone else first.

The pulse in my body throbbed as anger rolled through me, and when I kicked in the door of Benjamin Caruso's home, he snapped out of his slumber and sat up quickly on the side of the bed.

"Who's there?" he yelled as I floated out of the

shadows like an apparition. Benjamin's eyes widened, and terror struck across his face. "Who..." he fumbled with his words. "Who are you?"

I pulled the shotgun into the dim lighting so he could see it, and his worrying eyes dropped to the weapon.

"You've got some sins to make up for, Benjamin."

Sadness crept into his eyes, and then he nodded. "I knew this day would one day come."

"And yet, you didn't take precautions."

"Because when it's time to meet the reaper, does anyone have a chance of getting away?"

"Fair point. Lift your chin."

Sweat beaded across his forehead, and he closed his eyes and prayed profusely.

I tucked the shotgun under his chin and lodged the butt of the gun on the floor. Grabbing his hands, I place his pointing finger on the trigger and his teeth chattered as more sweat built up on his face.

"On the count of three, pull the trigger, and Benjamin, don't hesitate. It'll be worse if I do it."

His body trembled harder, and more prayers rolled from his tongue. On the dresser top, I set a recording.

"One..."

"Forgive me for my sins, I vow to thee, oh Father of the most high..."

"Two..."

"Sins forgiven, wash me with your spirit, oh Lord in..."

"Three..."

He opened his eyes, sucked in his final breath, and pulled the trigger.

POW!

Benjamin's body lunged backward from the blast; his brains splattered against the wall as he landed in the middle of the bed.

I let the recording run for another second before stopping it and sending it to Penelope.

21

Penelope

An hour later

I held on to a butcher knife and tucked myself farther under the covers. It had been storming for hours, and my anxiety was through the roof. Something about the night's storm seemed different—harsher, unrelenting—but I shook it off, telling myself it was only my imagination.

Another round of thunder and my heart was racing. *God, why couldn't I get over this?* I was a grown woman. No one was coming after me. Why couldn't I pull myself together?

I was frustrated enough that I hung my head and tapped the blade against my forehead.

"Come on, Penelope," I whispered.

The ringing of my cell phone pulled me out of my panic long enough to reach for my phone and open the text from a four-digit code number.

A video began playing. A man was sitting on the edge of the bed with a shotgun underneath his throat.

My eyes widened. "What the fuck is this?" I murmured, and that's when the muttering from his voice took my breath away.

I froze, squinted, and got closer to the video.

"Oh, my God..."

I pulled the covers from my head and folded my legs underneath me. There was another voice in the background that sounded like...a countdown?

The closer the voice got to one, the more Uncle Benjamin prayed. My heart slammed in my chest when the gun went off.

"Oh, my God!" I covered my mouth as every nerve in my body jumped, and for a few seconds, all was still and quiet, and then the recording cut off.

I fisted the phone in my hand when thunder rippled through the heavens, and lightning struck in front of my window, illuminating the room.

"Aaaaaah!" I screamed as a shadow appeared in my doorway, my pulse now slamming recklessly.

Dominic entered the room stealthily, and I breathed a sigh of relief and cried simultaneously. He scooped me into his arms and rocked me while holding me tight.

"You never have to worry about him or the storms, ever."

I snapped my head back, and more tears fell down my face. "It was you?"

He stared at me.

"Counting?"

He didn't respond, and I covered my mouth, unable to wrap my head around how I felt about this revelation.

"I..."

"You told me not to get him in trouble. And I told you I couldn't do that. If you want me to apologize, I can't do that either. I don't regret it, and I'd do it again if it were possible."

I stared at him, wide-eyed. I thought of my parents, and a knot formed in my throat, but then, something else filled me—relief. As much as I wanted to hurt for my parents who'd lost a brother, I couldn't.

"I have to go," he said.

"What? Why?"

His gaze combed over me, caressing me everywhere, connecting and commanding me without saying a word.

He reached for my chin, pinched me there, then slipped his hand at the nape of my neck and drew me in for a hot, hungry, stimulating kiss.

Our hearts banged between our chests, and I was further aroused, but he drew back and unraveled us and stood up.

"Maybe in another life," he said.

"Dominic?"

He left as quickly as he came, and once I'd come out of my shock and went after him, he was gone.

OVER THE NEXT FEW DAYS, Dominic had been absent from campus. I was worried about him; his disappearance kept me awake at night and distracted during the day.

The weather seemed increasingly cold, as if winter knew no bounds and would remain long after the season had ended.

I strolled solemnly across campus and paused before crossing to avoid getting run over like I did the day I met Dominic. That memory was all it took to put me back in a trance, but I blinked out of it when a Lincoln Continental drove in front of me and stopped.

My heart raced as I hoped Dominic had changed his mind and left the shadows.

The window rolled down, and my eyes widened to see my grandfather, Riccardo Niccolò, the don of the Niccolò Cartel, in front of me.

I spoke in Italian as that was the only language he cared to speak.

"What happened?"

"Granddaughter, it is time for me to pull you out."

The back door unlocked. "Get in."

Forbidden Obsession

To be continued...

Sneak Peek

Get a look inside chapter one of *Relentless Pursuit –
Boneless Redemption* Book Two on the next page!

Chapter One
Penelope

Large black umbrellas covered the heads of everyone in attendance at Uncle Benjamin's funeral. Fat raindrops dropped in a heavy shower, and I couldn't be certain, but it didn't make sense for the heavens to cry today.

The world had lost a piece of shit—a son of a bitch—a rapist—a pedophile.

The sky should've been bright, the sun shining, flowers growing in every budding garden across the globe.

Instead, we stood still. Family I hadn't seen in years and family I never knew I had. Not a single person shed a tear. Faces were stoic, weary, confused by his "suicide," but not too much saddened.

It had been two weeks since his death. Authorities immediately called it a suicide due to the nature of his death and the way Benjamin was found. Only I knew the truth.

When I first saw the recording, my immediate response was shock.

Then I realized it had happened at the hands of my academic advisor—my professor—my lover—my love...the shock soared tenfold.

I sighed as traces of water slipped through my umbrella and pelted my coat sleeves. In the short distance, a gray bus drove onto the gravel, parked, and all heads turned to the new arrivals.

I read the words on the side of the bus: Federal Bureau Detention Center.

My eyes widened, and I turned to face the transport. The doors opened, and two uniformed inmates were ushered off.

When their heads lifted, I gasped, and tears clouded my vision.

My father looked as if he'd aged twenty years. Gray hair sprouted from his head, spiked and wet like he used to wear it when it was the same golden-brown as mine. His once-shining eyes were dull, deep-set, and weary. He didn't appear to be the man who once took on the entire world. Not even close.

By his side, my eyes fluttered to my mother. A wound inside me seemed to split open as I perused her. I was closer to her when she left—when she chose a life of crime over me. And while I thought I was over it, seeing her now brought a heavy sadness that squeezed my heart.

Her once shoulder-length blonde hair was black, cut short to her ears, and stringy. An officer yanked them apart and pushed them forward, and I twitched every time he touched them.

Had they been abused?

My throat tightened, and without thinking, I wiggled through the group and walked at a fast pace in their direction.

When I broke through the crowd, their eyes turned to me just as another officer cut me off, stepping in my line of sight.

"Turn around and go back to your seat."

"Or you'll do what?"

He glared at me. "Do as I said, girl, or you'll wish you did."

My eyes widened. "Is that a threat?"

He whistled, and the guard who stood by my parents pushed them in their backs. "On your knees!"

My parents kneeled, and my heart squeezed. I glared back at the officer but took a few steps back, remaining outside the crowd to watch them.

The officer turned back and nodded, and the guard at their side shouted.

"On your feet!"

They stood up, and it was the first time I noticed the handcuffs linked in front of them. Their gray and orange jumpsuits were soggy at the knee area down, and I grimaced, knowing it was my fault.

"You could let me speak to them."

The officer turned back to me and stared but didn't respond.

"It's not as if they're going anywhere."

He remained silent but continued to glare.

"It's a funeral, for God's sake. What is wrong with you?"

"Your issue is you think I give a fuck. You only see my face because I clocked in this morning. Suck my dick and fuck your funeral."

I shook my head. "You need to grow up. One day, you'll be here. Everyone has a day."

"Yeah? And I hope you're not there because I'll ignore you again." Wretched laughter sprang from his mouth, and I rolled my eyes and looked back at my parents, who watched our exchange.

A tiny curve was etched on my mother's lips, and she mouthed, *I love you.* Tears streamed down my face, and my father nodded—his way of greeting me.

"At this time, you may come up in a line to say your final goodbyes," the officiant said.

Row by row, the family dropped their roses on the casket and said their peace. I remained standing in my spot when a calming balm of warmth settled over me. I turned my head to look behind me, my gaze scanning past the awaiting cars—by the gathering of trees—to the headstones further in the distance.

I could not see him, but I felt him.

Dominic.

I couldn't explain why I knew he was there, or why I knew he'd been at the campus award ceremony, or why I felt him when I was grocery shopping, but I was sure he lurked, and why he remained hidden from me still puzzled me at this very moment.

I turned back as someone approached me, my gaze falling on Uncle Dexter. He sighed, opened his arms, and pulled me in for a hug. "It's just me and you now."

I embraced him and pulled back. "It's been me and you for a long time, Uncle Dexter."

He nodded. "I'm sorry I don't come around often enough."

"You're busy. I understand."

"It's no excuse. I'll try to change that."

"Don't worry about it. It appears I'll be busy soon, too." He frowned. "Why?"

"I'm..." I sighed and rubbed my temples. "Grandpa wants me to, to..."

Uncle Dexter frowned and shook his head. "What does that son of a bitch want now?"

The onslaught of a headache suddenly arose as I recalled the argument with my grandfather—the don of the Niccolò Cartel.

"*What does that mean? I have a life now. You can't just pull me out of it.*"

"*I can and I will. Now get in the car, and don't make me repeat myself.*"

"*No. I have something to do. Next time, call first, and we can schedule an appointment.*"

"*Get in the car, or I'll have that boy toy you've been messing around with nailed to a stake!*"

My eyes widened, and I shook with anger. I didn't believe Dominic was the type who could be taken down easily, so while I wanted to call my grandfather's bluff, I knew Riccardo Niccolò was the type to try.

Gritting my teeth, I opened the back door, climbed inside, and slammed the door as the driver drove off.

"Is it that bad?"

I blinked from my thoughts and focused on Uncle Dexter. Nodding, I sighed. "Unfortunately, it is."

He grimaced. "Tell me what it is, and I'll tell Riccardo to go to hell."

I smirked. "Thanks, but I don't want you involved."

"Why? I'm not afraid of your grandfather. He's not the only one who has connections."

I laughed lightly. "I don't think there's anything the armed forces can do in this situation, Uncle Dexter."

"I beg to differ."

I rubbed my lips together and caught the guard ushering my mom and dad forward to get their final view of their brother.

"Did you know they'd be here today?"

He glanced back at them then back to me. "I knew there was a possibility. Otherwise, your uncle would've been buried last week."

"How did they find out?"

"The way we all did. The news."

I nodded and sighed, unable to take my eyes off them.

"How'd they end up together? Aren't they in separate facilities?"

"They're in the same prison on different sides. Female and male detention centers are combined in one. They most likely shoved them both on the same transport because they were coming to the same place for the same reason."

"Hmph."

"What's going on in that head of yours?"

My father leaned over the casket and wept. I turned my eyes from them, feeling sorry for his loss but glad the loss had happened. It was a wretched thing to wrestle with.

"Nothing."

Uncle Dexter peered at me. "Doesn't seem like nothing."

I peered back. "Are you inside my head now?"

"I don't need to be. I know you well enough to know when something is on your mind."

"Everything is on my mind. My parents, Grandpa's dubious plans, Dominic." I shook my head. "Some days I feel like I'm losing my mind."

"Who's Dominic?"

I froze, frowned, and pulled back a step. "Did I say Dominic?"

"Yes. Who is he?"

I shook my head. "I misspoke."

"You're much like me in the aspect that you hide so much from loved ones."

"Which loved ones? You? Them? Because you guys are all I have besides Grandfather, and none of you are available. So, just which loved ones am I hiding things from?"

"I said I would come around more, Penelope. I apologized, okay?"

I let out an exasperated sigh. "It's not about you. It's just..." I sucked my teeth. "I don't know. Forget about it."

My father was yanked away from the casket and ushered back the way they'd come. The graveyard was empty now except for my parents, Uncle Dexter, the guards, and the officiant.

Benjamin's coffin was lowered, and as my parents walked past me, I dropped my umbrella and took off into a sprint.

"Penelope, no!" Uncle Dexter shouted, but I was too

far gone. They were so close, closer than I'd been in a decade. They paused walking, and my father headbutted the guard while my mother tripped the other.

It was all I needed. I lunged into them, my arms swinging around their necks simultaneously.

"Mom! Dad!"

I kissed them—one, then the other, repeatedly as I cried tears of joy. "I love you so much. I miss you so much!"

We all put our lips together and kissed. They couldn't hug me, but we pushed our bodies together, and I squeezed them as tight as I could. My heart thrummed wildly. It was a moment of bliss I could bottle up and keep with me forever.

"We love you, baby," they said in unison.

"I'm sorry. I had to do it. I know you'll be in trouble, but I had to!"

"Don't be sorry," my father said. "Fuck them and everyone else."

My mother nodded. "We're not going down without a fight. You know us."

I laughed, and we hugged when something heavy struck my back, and pain ricocheted through my body.

"Aaaah!"

All three of us fell to the ground, and boots were shoved at our sides as we were kicked.

Shouts from my Uncle Dexter on the sidelines could be heard as he cursed at the officers who beat us. But he didn't move, most likely for fear that he would be reprimanded by his lieutenant and receive a dishonorable discharge.

I didn't blame him for it. I didn't blame anyone but myself, and as the pain continued to escalate in my body from their continuous kicks, I pulled my body into a fetal position and waited for it to stop.

SUBSCRIBE to my newsletter and get your bookish updates!

Ready for book two? Get it, now!

Made in the USA
Columbia, SC
03 February 2024

30995119R00122